To all those bri.   be they medical secretaries (the lifeblood of the NHS), porters, cleaners, nurses, midwives, sonographers, ward receptionists (without whom the wards would collapse), doctors, caterers (thank god for the caterers), and anyone else I haven't mentioned, working at the NHS coalface, who give their all and more for our patients every day of their working lives.

HOSPITAL
BLUES

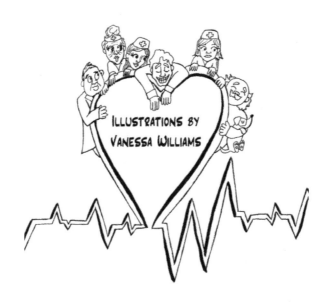

ILLUSTRATIONS BY
VANESSA WILLIAMS

BY

S R WATERMEYER

CONTENTS

ACKNOWLEDGMENTS

To Ali – best wife in the world (and best cook!)

CHAPTER 1

In a small, dark side room of the psychiatric wing, Richard or 'Dick' Chambers sat in front of his psychiatrist extolling the virtues of flying. The female psychiatrist rolled her not unattractive eyes skyward and let Dick continue his solo discourse as she carefully noted down the more salient features of his delusional state.

"Doc, I know that you know that I can fly. I have miniature rockets lodged in my heels and these give me an ability to fly at the speed of sound. Are you from the Ministry of Defence? 'Cos if you are, the answer is, yes. Queen and Country and all that. Whatever top-secret mission, however dangerous… I am your man. Dick Chambers to the rescue."

The psychiatrist looked down at her notes and enquired, "Dick, how long have you had the ability to fly at the speed of sound?"

"Do you know what, Doc, I think it was…" Dick started to answer the question then changed tack. "My God, you are gorgeous, how long have you had legs up to your neck? Oops, I'm sorry. Shouldn't be naughty, but you are rampantly good looking even for a psychiatrist… or are you from the MoD? Do you fancy a supersonic flight around Cardiff? I'll show you all the sights. The earth will move."

"That's very kind, Dick, but I might give that a miss. Please can we get back to the point – how long have you been able to fly?" The psychiatrist sat with her shapely legs crossed, skirt just above her knees, and in fairness looked pretty sumptuous.

Dick couldn't help himself. "I've been flying since I was 22, ex-RAF you know, and will you marry me?"

The problem was that Dick Chambers was indeed a previous fast jet pilot in the Royal Air Force and could indeed fly conventional aircraft. It was just his claim that he could take to the skies powered only by the supersonic rockets in his heels that worried his doctor.

He had been brought into the psychiatric unit via A&E after the police had been called to the city centre to deal with a maniac flapping his arms whilst running down the centre of the High Street, shouting, "Chocks away!" The police officer who had apprehended him and brought him to hospital stated that he had remained entirely amiable throughout his whole psychotic episode – they were worried much more about his well-being than that of the general public to whom they felt he posed absolutely no risk. The A&E staff were only too pleased to see Dick, since up to that point they had had to deal with abusive drunks, complainants with nothing but a simple cold, a rather delicate lady with a spot on her bum and a man complaining of discomfort from the potato residing in his back passage (he had apparently been peeling spuds in the bath and one had slipped in). The staff had found Dick particularly affable when he had threatened to 'duff up' a rather ferocious-looking, muscular, six-foot skinhead for being rude and aggressive to the young receptionist. With fists clenched and raised, Dick danced around the bully shouting, "Do you want a bit of this then? I'll give you a good smacking! Now apologise to this young lady or else!" To everyone's amazement the skinhead duly burst into tears and apologised profusely to the stunned receptionist. Following his chastisement the young man acted like Larry the Lamb, courtesy and politeness being his middle names.

Dick's lack of inhibitions allowed him to freely

express his opinions and when he instructed the rather precious lady with the spot on her arse to 'get a life and stop wasting people's time' the A&E staff had definitely warmed to him. Following these vocal incidents, they had completely taken him to their hearts, but more was to come to endear him to them. Dick had slipped out unnoticed from behind one of the curtained cubicles as the staff had rushed off to deal with a cardiac arrest and escaping to the hospital canteen, he had bought 20 cups of coffee and 20 welsh cakes. He managed to acquire a canteen trolley to transport the refreshments back to A&E where he duly ordered everyone to cease work for 'Coffee, Cakes and a Cuddle'. The delighted A&E staff accordingly obeyed and for 20 minutes everyone had a well-earned break before continuing with their ongoing harrowing shifts. Dick Chambers was diagnosed with a psychotic manic episode and merrily went off to the department of psychiatry humming the theme to 'Top Gun'.

The young female psychiatrist looked up from her the brief notes detailing Dick's admission and viewed this rather lovely chap. He was 59 years old, relatively well presented for a fellow who had not slept for three days, and was clearly articulate and bright, with a wonderful charming manner. She noted that there was absolutely no previous record of past medical or psychiatric history – either on paper or computerised, which was odd since most psychiatric patients of his age would have had some previous episode or admission. From what could be pieced together, the last time Dick had been seen or spoken to by a medic was some 20 years previously, when he had been a Squadron Leader in the RAF and had undeniably flown Tornado fast jet aircraft. The man had never had a day's illness in his life. So what had precipitated this episode of acute mania?

Dick continued his rambling dialogue. "So Doc, here is a question for you... why did you do psychiatry? Are you dotty or is there someone in your family who's barking? You know, it's a bit like dermatologists... most of them have had really bad, Rocky-Horror-Show acne in the past and become dermatologists to cure themselves. I wonder why people become willy doctors and bum doctors. If you ask me, they are the ones who need to see a quack, not me. Oh, and are you sure you don't want to get hitched?"

"Dick..." The psychiatrist managed to get a word in.

"Yes my lovely... oops... sorry, yes Doctor."

"Has there ever been a Mrs Chambers and if so

where is she now?" the psychiatrist gently probed. The question affected Dick as if he had been shot at point-blank range. In the passage of a few seconds he seemed like a different man.

"Yes," he whispered in a voice that was only just audible, "but she's gone now." His face fell, he looked ashen. His verbal ramblings ceased. It was the first time in three days that he had stopped talking. When he looked up at the psychiatrist, his eyes were full of tears that started to tumble down his cheeks and he suddenly looked old, vulnerable and exhausted. Then Dick Chambers started to weep, he wept so that the depth of his grief filled the room and the transition from an ebullient, confident and energetic human being to a hollow vessel of pain was complete. The young psychiatrist had unwittingly begun to uncover the reason for Dick's current psychiatric illness, but now the consultation could go no further, for Dick Chambers was inconsolable. The young female doctor gently and kindly had him escorted and transferred to the psychiatric ward of the hospital where he was given a much needed tranquiliser. In the safety of this new refuge and suitably medicated, he then proceeded to sleep for the first time in three days – a deep, long-overdue, drug-induced sleep that he so badly needed.

*

After making further enquiries, the psychiatric team slowly pieced together the core events of Dick Chambers' life, although of course they could never know any of the intimate details unless he shared them. Over time, and after diligent research and gentle questioning, the more pertinent and significant moments of their patient's previous existence was revealed. He had never suffered with any psychiatric or medical disorder. He had been born into a middle-class family, and had a happy childhood. From an early age he knew that he wanted to fly, it was his passion and his raison d'être. He excelled at school, becoming head boy, and achieved the A-levels he needed for direct entry into the Royal Air Force to learn to fly. After receiving the prize for best overall cadet at Initial Officer Training at the prestigious RAF College, Cranwell, Dick Chambers lived his passion and before long he was a trainee pilot, winning all and every flying award. In record time the young officer had obtained his wings, and now concentrated on his other passion in life, his childhood sweetheart, Ann O'Reilly.

They had met on the first day of senior school. Dick had been pushed over in the playground by an older boy, a well-known bully who randomly picked on younger boys and took delight in tormenting them.

Ann had walked over to where Dick had lain, his knees grazed and bleeding. She had given him the biggest and most wonderful smile, then offered an outstretched hand and pulled him up off the concrete playground. The bully had taken exception to this act of kindness and grabbing Ann's hair had started to drag her around the playground. Dick for the first time in his young life had felt raw fury at such despicable behaviour. He had flown at the older boy with teeth gritted and fists flying. The bully was floored both by the onslaught of a frenzy of punches and by the complete shock that a lad half his size would dare to confront him. A great cheer went up in the playground as Dick jumped on the felled bully and continued to hit him as hard and as fast as he could. Only after the teacher on duty had pulled Dick off did the assault stop. Needless to say, from that day onwards, the bullying in the playground ceased and young Dick Chambers and Ann O'Reilly were inseparable.

With his future flying career sorted, Dick determined to marry his long-term childhood sweetheart. It was the most natural progression in the world and after Ann had readily agreed to his enthusiastic proposal, the young couple had shared a joyous wedding. Six months after their marriage, they were transferred to a front-line fast jet station in

Germany, where Dick served with distinction. After 16 years in the military with an exemplary record, he retired and went to work for a civilian airline, safely flying tourists around the world. The couple had a good life and were devoted to each other. The one regret in their otherwise perfect marriage was that they were unable to have children. They had seen medical experts, undergone numerous IVF treatments but all to no avail. It might have broken some marriages, but made the two of them even more dedicated and caring of each other. Their subsequent life was a happy one with much daft activity and joyful laughter with friends and extended family, and this happy equilibrium had lasted for many years.

Then two years ago disaster had struck and everything had changed. Ann had found a lump in her breast and was diagnosed with cancer. Dick had immediately stopped flying around the world to spend more time with and look after the woman that he loved. He was there to kiss her tenderly before she went into theatre for surgery, he was there when she opened her eyes after the anaesthetic had worn off and he held her when she endured the sickness and hair loss induced by chemotherapy. For a short time after her treatment, the couple fulfilled her bucket list – they travelled to exotic locations, danced on a tropical beach at midnight, drank champagne in a bubbling hot-tub in the snow, holding each other close, laughing and loving. But the cancer returned. He fed her, washed her, and clothed her. He held her close at night and comforted her when no one else could. He simply loved her more than anything else in the world.

When Ann died, Dick appeared initially to cope. He had always been a strong character, but after the organisation of her funeral, an event full of the celebration of her life with plenty of laughter at some of the wonderful memories they had shared, as well as sorrow – Dick went downhill. He suddenly no longer needed to be her rock, no longer needed to be strong. He tried to cope being without her, taking long walks along the river, reading, exercising at the local gym, and getting involved in local charities, but he had never felt so alone. He became enveloped in a fog of sadness and then depression. It was so alien to him. He had always been active, jovial and outgoing, but his wife's death had hit him like a runaway juggernaut and now it sapped him of his own joy for life. Then one morning, it happened – he couldn't explain it but he had loads of energy, was talkative in the extreme, and so his manic phase started – of course his previous flying career subconsciously influenced the choice of his psychotic delusions, and the flying, rocket-propelled man was his grandiose misconception. The trouble was that if he continued to believe this and enacted it, it would certainly lead to his own demise and possibly risk harming others in the process.

His psychiatrist diagnosed Dick Chambers with manic depression, the likely precipitating factor being the death of his beloved wife. After the much needed tranquilliser, he was started on both antipsychotic and mood stabilising medication. However, it would take time for these drugs to really kick in. A few days after Dick had awoken from the effect of the tranquiliser, he was still in the manic phase of his illness, but refreshed from all the lovely sleep and with bags of energy. When he found the door to the psychiatric ward was locked and elaborate security mechanisms were in place to prevent him from leaving, he likened it to being a prisoner of war and resolved to make his escape. He studied the time of meals, coffee breaks, shift changes, and times at which the staff would be the least alert. He identified one of the more forgetful mental health nurses and noticed the numbers on the back of her hand – written hastily with a biro to compensate for her appalling memory. The five-digit numbers turned out to be the numerical codes for the door locks to the ward and the psychiatric unit.

Moreover, Dick had managed to steal a number of Valium tablets from a momentarily unattended drugs trolley which he would later use to facilitate his plan.

Dick chose his time to escape with military precision. It was late afternoon, and all the ward rounds had been completed. Lunch provided a sleepy state such that the overworked, sparse nursing staff would be at their lowest ebb in terms of security. Moreover, the Valium tablets that had been ground down and surreptitiously sprinkled into their coffee aided the effect. Before long the entire duty psychiatric nursing team sat slouched in chairs, snoring their heads off. Dick made his move. He had managed to acquire a dark pair of trousers and black turtle-neck pullover from the staff lockers, so that he resembled an aged MI5 spy, making his way out of enemy territory. The five-digit door codes obeyed his input and Dick said a quiet thank you to the forgetful psychiatric nurse who had written them on the back of her hand. Before he knew it, Dick had reached the main entrance vestibule of the psychiatric unit without raising any suspicion. He calmly walked past the information desk, where the receptionist and attending security guard gave him a quizzical look.

"Excuse me, sir, you'll need to sign out," the receptionist politely requested from behind the desk.

Dick took no notice and quickened his pace towards the front door. "Excuse me, sir, but we need you to sign out, you are not allowed to leave without…"

But Dick was gone. He ran as if his life depended on it. Alarms sounded behind him, followed by shouts of irate security staff. He turned to see a rather large, red-faced and already out of breath security guard giving chase. The sound of thumping footsteps behind him concentrated his mind, but he was still pretty agile for a bloke of 59 years of age and his recent visits to the gym now paid off. He soon outpaced his rather stout pursuer, but as he ran across the hospital car park and off the premises, he knew that others would soon be on his tail.

Behind the hospital were rows of delightful Victorian terraced houses, and at the back of these homes, a series of lanes with rows of back gates and the occasional garage. Although he had by now completely lost the psychiatric security guard, who had fallen well behind and had likely given up the pursuit, Dick heard the unmistakeable warble of a police car siren and it was fast approaching. The old fellow darted into one of the lanes behind the Victorian terraces and made haste along their cobbled surface. He passed a series of back garden gates, some with rather inhospitable barbed wire on the top and along their garden walls. He ran past a number of brightly coloured garage doors, until panting and out of breath he doubled over, hands on knees, and stopped. The warbling of the police siren was very close now. Dick looked up. On the opposite side of the lane, a pretty, pink, wooden back gate caught his eye and it was just low enough for him to scramble over as well as being devoid of barbed wire. However, nailed to the top of the gate, was a sign, *'Beware of the Dog'*.

Dick's manic brain conjured up images of a pack of growling, teeth-baring Alsatians tearing into the flesh of any would-be intruder – but he was escaping the enemy and would have to take his chances. As the police car turned into the back lane, Dick hurled himself over the pretty pink back gate.

Better to be ripped apart by a ferocious dog than be recaptured by the enemy, he thought. With eyes closed and breath held, he landed with a thump on the other side of the gate. No fangs ripping out his throat yet. After a few seconds, he tentatively opened one eye. A small patch of manicured lawn with a neat path and flower beds filled with colour and the most glorious of scents struck his senses. There was a small pond with a decorative gurgling water feature, the sound of which was somewhat restorative. The flagstoned path led to the back door of the house, the lower half of which framed what looked like a dog flap. The back of the little Victorian terrace was brightly painted and hanging baskets added to the impression of tranquillity and order. Dick relaxed just a little, then there was a growl from inside the house and the flap flew open. From it, running at full pace emerged a little bundle of fighting fury. Geoffrey, the Jack Russell terrier, was not one to be trifled with and *no one* entered his back yard without the express permission of his beloved owner.

With snarling teeth he charged towards the uninvited intruder and as Dick turned around and ducked away to protect himself, the little dog sunk his canines into Dick's rear end. The fact that his jaws were deeply embedded into Dick's quivering buttock meant that any barking was quickly subdued and this together with Dick's rather impressive forced silence, meant that the passing police car failed to pick up any suspicious activity.

With the cessation of any police or security presence, Dick turned his attention to his by now, rather sore arse. Geoffrey's gleaming canines were still firmly embedded into their intended victim's bum and there was no way that the little dog was letting go. Sensing Geoffrey's determination, Dick could see only one solution to his current rather uncomfortable predicament. He stood up, and gingerly waddled painfully towards the pond before dunking his throbbing backside with attached dog into the water and towards some startled goldfish. Geoffrey, faced with either letting go of his foe or drowning to death whilst attached to his foe's arse, decided the former was preferable and released his formidable grip.

Dick exhaled a great sigh of relief. He heaved his rear end out of the pond, clutching the punctured skin and tooth marks on his aching behind. He turned and saw Geoffrey swimming around and around, unable to clamber out of the pool of water. The little dog started to whimper as he became more and more tired. Dick reflected on whether he should leave the mutt to drown, but he was not a cruel man, even in his manic state. Anyway he admired the little fellow for defending his patch so valiantly, so he fished Geoffrey out and placed him gently on the lawn to dry out and recover his breath.

The little dog lay panting on the soft lush grass and looking up at Dick now saw not an adversary, but a saviour. When he had recovered his breath, he toddled up to the psychiatric patient, tail wagging and if dogs could grin – Geoffrey was grinning. For his part, Dick looked into the little dog's eyes and his brain registered 'co-pilot'.

"Well old boy, I take my hat off to you… my arse is bloody sore and I have no doubt you are an excellent guard dog. You and I, we'd make good partners, don't you think? How about you and I go for a spot a flying? You can be my co-pilot. What do you say?" Dick spoke as if he were addressing an old military colleague. He noticed the name 'Geoffrey' on the little dog's collar. "You and me… Geoffrey?"

The little dog barked an affirmative and Dick, now completely ensconced in his manic mood, stood and saluted the hound. The hospital from where he had escaped, which consisted of a tower block with surrounding buildings, loomed large in front of them. He counted a good seven storeys high; the top of that building, Dick concluded, would make a good platform from which the two of them could launch… it seemed a good place to try out the rockets in his shoes.

Much to Dick's surprise and delight, Geoffrey had gone back into the house via the dog flap to retrieve his own lead which he now presented to his idol with a wagging tail. Dick duly consented and attaching the lead to Geoffrey's ornate collar, opened the pretty back gate from the inside and stepped out into the cobbled back lane. Man and dog walked in the direction of the hospital. As a pair, they were relatively inconspicuous – they just looked like a chap walking his dog.

It was an extraordinary feat for Geoffrey and Dick to get to the seventh floor of the hospital without being challenged. Dogs and busy hospitals don't usually suit each other in view of hygiene and the risks of infection. But hospital administrators, porters, nursing and medical staff ever busy and in their own worlds, largely ignored the pair as they made their way into the lift and their intended destination. It just so happened that the seventh floor was home to the surgical ward and just beyond the ward entrance there was a staircase that led up to the roof terrace. As they walked towards the stairwell, Mr Rick Donovan, a newly appointed consultant gynaecologist, exited the ward and spotted Dick and Geoffrey entering the stairwell.

"Ahhhh… excuse me, what on earth are you doing with a dog up here? Dogs are not allowed within the hospital premises and I certainly don't think you want to go up there… it's just the roof terrace and forgive me for saying so, sir, but you and your dog need to leave immediately. Please take the elevator to the ground floor and the exit and we'll say no more." Rick gently raised his voice to ensure that the transgressing member of the public and his pooch had definitely heard him. The gynaecologist paused as a number of his nurses came out of the surgical ward doors and looked in surprise at the little Jack Russell.

Dick was determined that the flying duo were not going to be put off their mission. Looking seriously down at the little dog, he whispered, "Leave this to me, partner." Dick's manic mind went into overdrive; he turned to Mr Donovan and in all seriousness barked out, "British Army, bomb squad, sir. This is my trusty sniffer dog, Geoffrey. He is a highly trained professional… but don't be alarmed. We have had reports of a nutter planting a suspect package on the roof terrace… just need to go and check it out."

Rick faltered for a few moments, confused by the insanity of what he was hearing. He had certainly never heard of a Jack Russell being employed by the British Army as a sniffer dog, and he felt that 'Geoffrey' was an unlikely name for such a professional canine.

Dick continued, "Don't worry, old chap, we won't be back this way anyhow, my sniffer dog co-pilot and I plan to thoroughly investigate and fly onwards."

"Pardon…?" Rick stuttered and was confused. He momentarily looked around at one of the nurses who was standing at the entrance to the surgical ward, tittering at the unfolding events.

The nurse laughed and then hastily added, "Oh my god, that's not a British Army sniffer dog, that's the ward sister's Jack Russell... his name is Geoffrey!"

Rick had heard enough; he turned to accost the unlikely pair, but Dick and Geoffrey were gone. They had pounded up the staircase, through an exit door and found themselves on the roof terrace in the open air. The sky had never looked so inviting. Rick stood almost dumbfounded. His brain couldn't quite make it out. Then a spark of intuition fired up as he remembered overhearing in the staff canteen the story of a manic depressive patient with flying delusion, who had spiked the psychiatric team's coffee before making a daring escape. Apparently the police had not found him and he was a significant danger to himself. "Oh God... it's him... and the roof terrace!" Rick cursed under his breath. "Why me... why is it always bloody well me?"

Rick yelled for help at the gaggle of nurses, telling them to ring security. Then he bounded, three steps at a time, up the stairwell that led to the roof terrace and burst out into the open air, seven floors up. The man and his little dog were teetering on the edge of the building. One arm was outstretched skyward ready for take-off, the other wrapped protectively around Geoffrey whom he held close to his chest. The little dog, sensing something was not quite right as they swayed on the ledge of the seven-storey building had started to whimper.

"It's alright my little friend, the first flight is bound to be a bit scary," Dick tried to reassure the little Jack Russell who remained unimpressed, but there was little he could now do. "For God and Country!" Dick shrieked, giving it his best, and leaped, Geoffrey under his arm, from the building's ledge.

Rick had sprinted the short distance towards the maniac and diving as if he were still in his rugby-playing days, caught him around the ankles just as Dick launched himself forward. Dick was not a small man and Rick had certainly ruptured something as he hit the floor, arms entangled around the aviator's ankles. He held on with all his might and then painfully pulled Dick back from the abyss.

The consultant gynaecologist saved the life of Mr. Dick Chambers that day and fortunately Dick never managed to try out the fantasy rockets in his feet. As for poor old Geoffrey, the aborted take-off jolted the little dog clean out of the arm of his co-pilot. As he descended, he howled a haunting wail on his way to a certain and rather undignified death. The little Jack Russell opened his bowels in terror, as he fell. Then for Geoffrey all went dark. The little dog's life was over, and his loss would change the life of his mistress for ever.

CHAPTER 2

It was one of those usual horrendous months in the cash-strapped, struggling to cope Welsh NHS, on a surgical ward called Bedlam. Joyce Evans had been the faithful ward sister, ruling her little domain with a fierce efficiency, yet kindly manner. But today, she was absent and her lack of presence was all too evident, exacerbating an already dire situation in the clinical environment. Sister Evans had worked for the NHS for 35 years and was looking forward to a well-deserved retirement. She epitomised the hardworking, caring, and no-nonsense ward sister in a blue uniform that everybody respected – her life was that hospital. However, like all human beings, Joyce also had her own foibles. For example, she had a propensity to fly off the handle whenever things were not done the way that *she* wanted. The junior doctors were terrified of her, as were her nursing colleagues, the ward receptionist, the cleaners, and even the tough tattooed porters. Whenever she became flustered, a nervous twitch appeared above her right eye and you knew that trouble was ahead. She lived around the corner from the hospital in a little Victorian terraced house, with a pretty back garden, complete with its own ornate pond. As well as being a regular churchgoer, she was a long-time member of the WRVS and was everything you would expect of a respectable, 55-year-old spinster. When she was not working, Joyce could be found tending to her garden or spending time with her one devoted companion in life, a feisty Jack Russell called Geoffrey.

Disaster had struck Joyce's stable and predictable existence. For the first time in living memory Joyce was not at her desk or marching around the ward barking orders – for she was apparently 'sick'. This unfortunate state of affairs followed the unexpected death of her faithful pooch, Geoffrey. The poor mutt had had the misfortune to be mistaken for a flying co-pilot by a noncompliant psychotic escapee who stole the unlucky canine and forced him over the edge of the seventh floor of her hospital. Far from being a co-pilot, Geoffrey acted like a stone and certainly dropped like one. A plucky gynaecologist had arrived in time to prevent the psychiatric patient from launching his ill-fated aeronautical enterprise, but alas for poor Geoffrey, the gynaecologist and subsequent security staff were too late. The little dog howled loudly during his descent and was heard by all and sundry. In addition, on his way down he evacuated his bowels, the contents of which landed on the chief executive's head as she exited the underground car park on foot.

On the day of these unfortunate events and preceding them, Joyce had been working hard as always on Bedlam ward, but then had developed an inexplicable sense of doom that something ghastly was about to happen. It certainly set off a florid bout of twitching of her right eye and forced her to take her leave. Her morbid intuition was that her Geoffrey was in grave danger and desperately needed her help. As things turned out, her extraordinary perception was entirely correct. The nursing staff were shocked to see her leaving the ward, but for once Joyce determined that she must put her own needs first and tend to her little dog. She ran out of the main entrance and passed the hospital car park. As she hastened home, she witnessed the astonishing sight of a flying turd floor the chief executive, who was subsequently covered in shit. At the same time and to her horror, a little bundle of fur landed adjacent with a sickening thud on hard, unforgiving ground. She knew instantly that it was Geoffrey and it broke her heart. She ran to where her little dog had fallen, gathered him in her arms then falling onto her knees, sobbed her heart out.

Staff and the general public gathered around her to try and comfort her. Even the chief executive, who had problems of her own, went over to see if she could help. Joyce took the little dog home and for the first few days just lay him in his dog bed, stroking the little corpse and talking to him. Finally, when he was as stiff as a board and starting to become a bit smelly, she saw fit to say goodbye to him with a dignified ceremony and burial in her garden.

Members of the WRVS attended Geoffrey's well-organised funeral and the outdoor service was conducted by Joyce's local vicar, in close proximity to the fishpond that only recently Geoffrey had swum in. In the days that followed the little dog's sudden demise, Joyce just couldn't return to work. She couldn't sleep, couldn't smile and started to lose weight. Her garden was left unattended, the goldfish in her pond unfed. Despite the efforts of many friends, she became unkempt and started to lose the will to live. Her GP visited and diagnosed a severe bout of depression requiring her emergency admission to the

Psychiatric Unit. Due to the endemic bed shortage, Joyce was placed on the same ward as the psychotic dog murderer, although of course she didn't know. She wandered around the ward in a fugue state and despite some heavy drugs and even electroconvulsive therapy, Joyce Evans failed to get better.

In addition to missing their nursing sister, Bedlam ward had suffered another enormous blow when the long-term receptionist snuffed it with a massive heart attack the day after Sister Joyce Evans had been relieved of her duties. The unfortunate demise of the receptionist resulted in chaos and as there was no replacement to collect and process patient notes, answer the multitudes of phone calls from relatives enquiring about their loved ones, or carry out all the administrative chores that were generated from inpatients' surgical admissions and discharges. The effective running of the ward was now in serious jeopardy, if not complete tatters. Within three days following the unforeseen departure of two of its key members of staff, Bedlam ward was just that... utter Bedlam. The repercussions were first noted when Mrs Williams, a rather large female patient, who was originally admitted to Bedlam ward with gallstones, was sent to the operating theatre for removal of her gangrenous left testicle. The Government had no choice but to step in. The chief executive was severely reprimanded by a rather red-faced Health Minister and the Health Board told to do better or else.

Within one week of the 'gangrenous testicle' incident, the previous two key members of staff had been replaced and much to the relief of the chief executive, the ward had started to resemble something of an orderly establishment once more. The new ward receptionist, an experienced 62-year-old and rather flirtatious grandmother called Phyllis Jones, had been there, done it all, and seen it all. Phyllis did not take any crap. She was dolled up to the eyeballs with rather colourful makeup, and walked with a playful gait. She loved men. But this was her only weakness. Otherwise she was efficient, confident and wonderful on the phone to worried relatives calling to ensure that their loved ones had had the right operation.

The other new member of staff, appointed at the same time, was the ward sister. She had been slightly more difficult to find on account of the UK-wide nursing shortage, but after some intense negotiation and a promotion, Miss Alicia Granger had been appointed. Alicia was of a quieter disposition than her ward receptionist colleague. She was significantly younger, demure and pretty. But most of all, despite her young age, she was competent. After two days on

Bedlam ward, she knew the name, history and blood pressure of every single patient in her care. She had established decent working patterns and relationships with all who worked under her charge, winning over the staff and patients alike. The cleaners were gently reminded and then praised for a job well done, the nursing staff took pleasure in being part of a well organised and clean ward – and the patients, for whom of course the whole show existed, absolutely loved her. After only a week following Sister Alicia's appointment, her greatest admirer and most outspoken advocate turned out to be Phyllis.

One morning, shortly after Alicia had started, a rather self-important and smug consultant arrived on the ward with his entourage of junior doctors, in order to carry out a ward round. The consultant's name was Mr Henry Horsham and he was known to be something of a tyrant especially to the nursing staff. Only a few weeks earlier on his ward round, he had reduced the accompanying junior staff nurse to tears after shouting at her and accusing her of being incompetent. Phyllis, who had been in post for only a few days at that point, witnessed the entire debacle. She didn't have a problem with anyone being chastised for laziness, or failing to care for the patients properly, but the manner in which Mr

Horsham spoke to the unfortunate nurse in front of a ward of patients was clearly unacceptable. Apart from anything else, Phyllis could not quite understand why the dressing down was necessary since the nurse appeared to know her patient well, and her care seemed satisfactory. Furthermore, Mr Horsham appeared to be revelling in and actually enjoying reprimanding his nursing colleague, belittling her in front of his junior doctors. Phyllis had decided there and then that the bastard was a bully. She knew too that the newly appointed Sister Alicia Granger would be on the bully's radar. Young, relatively inexperienced, although highly competent – Alicia would certainly be a target. Phyllis had warned Alicia, telling her of the bullying episode that had occurred in her absence, and the receptionist knew that Horsham would choose his time carefully.

Horsham always did a ward round at 0900 hours sharp on Monday, Wednesday and Friday. Early on one particular Wednesday morning, two members of staff had called in sick and as well as having to delegate and personally help carry out their work, Alicia had also been busy with a postoperative patient of Horsham's, who had bleeding internally. She had taken blood, put an intravenous drip in, kept the patient nil by mouth and called the necessary on-call surgical team to review. Usually, Alicia organised the patient notes for each consultant ward round in a neat pile, corresponding to their location on the ward. She would ensure that the observation and medication charts of each patient to be reviewed were placed at the foot of each bed. This was to ensure a smooth and effective ward round. But this particular morning, the hectic ward and lack of staff meant that she had not managed to carry this out. To her horror, Horsham arrived with his entourage at 0900 hours precisely and he now stood, red-faced at the patient notes trolley, tapping his fingers impatiently.

"Sister Granger, am I expected to stand here waiting to do my round while you mess around with commodes? Where are my patients' notes?" Horsham raised his voice in a condescending manner. He knew that this was the morning to strike. He wanted to bring down this new ward sister a peg or two and he was going to relish every moment of it.

"Come on, come on, do you think that I've got all day…?" Horsham was starting to enjoy himself, and his entourage smelling the hint of blood had started to titter and smirk.

"Ohh… um… Mr Horsham, I'm so sorry… I'm afraid that…" Alicia was interrupted as Phyllis calmly placed a pile of notes in front of her and a rather startled Horsham. The grins were wiped off the faces of both Horsham and his team.

"As you asked, Sister… the notes for Mr Horsham's patients. In addition, as you requested the observation charts for each of his patients are enclosed and have all been done within the last 15 minutes." Phyllis had a naughty twinkle in her eye that caught Alicia's attention.

Alicia laughed inside and mimed, "Thank you," to her wonderful receptionist. She felt invigorated and confident, and to the amazement of the by now small gathering of ward staff, looked directly at Horsham and said, "Here are the notes, Mr Horsham… Oh and by the way, just to keep you up to date, one of your patients, a Mrs Williams… you operated on her yesterday. Her blood pressure has dropped, her pulse is rapid and I think she is bleeding internally – I would be grateful if you could review her first, I think she might need to go back to theatre."

Horsham responded furiously, "What rubbish, my patients never bleed postoperatively, and I certainly do not need to be told by a *nurse* when to take anyone back to theatre." The ward staff and Horsham's team looked to Alicia to see how she would respond and she was magnificent.

"Oh Mr Horsham, that is a shame since prior to your arrival, I requested the on-call surgical team to review Mrs Williams. They agreed with this *nurse* and also felt that this patient was bleeding internally following you operating on her."

Horsham was starting now to look rather uncomfortable.

"Furthermore, Mr Horsham, the CT scan that she returned from just 10 minutes ago has indicated that she has a belly full of blood. So may I again humbly request that you and your team review her first and make a decision before an incident becomes a tragedy. Staff nurse will accompany you with the necessary notes and charts. I am afraid that I have other things to attend to on my ward. Good morning." With that, Sister Alicia Granger turned and walked away from the arrogance of the dumbfounded consultant surgeon. The ward staff, especially Phyllis, were grinning from ear to ear and quietly applauding their new ward sister. Horsham, for the first time in his life obeyed a clearly competent nursing colleague and to his credit realised what a prig he had been.

"Oh… um… thank you, Sister." It was not only the ward staff who had grown to respect this new young, demure and competent ward sister, Horsham himself was shocked to find himself respecting her and dare he think it, but she had grown in stature in his eyes – not one to be trifled with. As the old surgeon found himself glaring admiringly at the new ward sister, the new ward receptionist for her part felt a stirring in her loins when she looked up again at Horsham… He was commanding, yet with a hint of humility when it was deserved. Phyllis rolled her heavily made up eyes to look up and down seductively at him. The old boy caught her adoring eye and embarrassed, he quickly looked away. Horsham ordered his team to start the ward round, first stop the patient that Sister Granger had pointed out. Then he surreptitiously glanced back at Phyllis and again held her indulgent eye. For the second time that morning found himself caught off guard, being both bewildered and surprised.

Sitting quietly in the corner of the ward, mulling over his patients' notes, was the newly appointed consultant gynaecologist, Mr Rick Donovan. He had just about recovered from his life-saving, rugby-tackling antics on the roof terrace of the hospital. Rick knew that Horsham could sometimes be a miserable old bastard, but he did have his good points. The gynaecologist quietly witnessed the whole show and noted Phyllis's seductive gaze, as well as Horsham's rather red complexion. He inwardly chuckled to himself. But more than that, he glanced again at the young ward sister and realised how wholeheartedly impressed he was.

CHAPTER 3

It was early evening and Rick Donovan had just arrived home. A removal van was parked outside his next-door neighbour's house, with men carrying in bits of furniture and multitudes of boxes.

"Ah, the arrival of new neighbours. I wonder what they are like, although I will miss dear old Enid, she was the best neighbour ever," Rick contemplated to himself as he parked his car a safe distance away from the removal men and their van. He was tired so didn't stop to welcome his new neighbour or neighbours who must have been inside unpacking. "They are probably busy… I'll catch up later and welcome them," he rationalised to himself.

It had been a difficult day. He went to the fridge, cracked opened a beer and then headed upstairs where he ran himself a deep muscle relaxant bubble bath. Rick immersed himself in the tub and sighed with pleasure as the hot water and foam infiltrated his weary limbs. He took a swig of the cold beer, closed his eyes and started to drift off.

In this state of wellbeing, Rick's mind was free to contemplate. Although he could well afford to do so, Rick hadn't moved from his two-up, two-down, little terraced house in Cardiff. He loved it here, with the pub around the corner and the salt-of-the-earth neighbours, although, there had been some sadness surrounding his previous next-door neighbour, Miss Enid Jones and her pint-size dog, Molly. Now Enid was gone, Rick had realised how close he had become to the old girl. He had even started to do little jobs around her house for her as she had become older and more fragile. More recently, she had suffered quite a severe stroke and had been moved to a nursing home, thus leaving the house next door vacant. A new family had been found for Molly and apparently they adored the little dog, and on occasions took her to see her former mistress, much to Enid's joy and delight. The 'For Sale' sign that went up shortly after her move, signified the end of an era, and the whole street were holding their breaths to see who would buy Enid's house and so who would be their new neighbour.

The little terrace needed a lot of work and updating and initially there seemed to have been only a modest interest from potential buyers. But then the inevitable 'Sold' sign went up and that was that. Rick, for his part had continued to visit Enid in the nursing home, taking her flowers and her favourite chocolates, but he was saddened by her decline. As fond of her as he was, their relationship had not always been easy and Enid had not always been a wonderful next-door neighbour. In the early days the two of them had had a few altercations as Enid had been outspoken and formidable to say the least, with a religious bent verging on the extreme. Rick, particularly in the early days, had been chastised by the old girl on account of his irreligious and blasphemous ways. It didn't help that the walls between the neighbours' terrace houses were not soundproof, and that Enid had had a keen ear, particularly for bad language and indeed for physical activity, which proved slightly tricky when Rick had been entertaining a voluptuous and over vociferous lady friend. The prayer meetings that the old girl had held had disturbed Rick's sleep, which hacked him off when he had had a gruelling night on call. Good neighbourly relations had not been helped when Enid's faithful little mongrel, Molly, had sunk her teeth into Rick on at least one occasion.

The unfortunate situation had been made immeasurably worse when Rick had in desperation 'borrowed' the old lady's Mini in order to get to the hospital in the middle of the night. The fact that his own car had been stolen and he needed to get to the hospital in an emergency to save a young woman's life had been disbelieved. In fact Enid hadn't even believed that Rick was a doctor. She had referred to him as 'that young hooligan' when he had knocked on her door in the middle of the night, taken her car keys from the key hook just inside her hall and disappeared with her car, claiming a dying patient needed him. It was then that she flipped.

It was the straw that broke the camel's back. Enid had seen Rick's actions as bloody minded theft and the taking advantage of an old lady. She had immediately reported him to the police and the hunt was on. A police patrol car had noticed Enid's speeding Mini heading in the direction of the hospital and blue lights had flashed, sirens wailed, but Rick had put his foot down and somehow the ancient little motor had done its duty. Rick had managed to get to the hospital, with the engine screaming and tyres screeching. He had abandoned the little car and ran, as if his own life had depended upon it, into the hospital and up to the operating theatre where his more than worried team were waiting for him. The young woman in question had bled litres of blood from a ruptured ectopic pregnancy and was now lying on the operating table in a critical state. Rick had scrubbed up, donned his operating blues and still panting from his run to the operating theatre had performed lifesaving surgery. Rick's colleagues had breathed a sigh of relief and then to them at least, the unthinkable had happened – Rick had been arrested as he walked out of the operating theatre. To the incredulity and anger of his colleagues he had been whisked away in handcuffs and held in a police cell overnight.

During this stressful time, Rick had been surprised by the wonderful level of support he had received from his medical colleagues. In particular, his mentor and consultant boss, Sir John Rawarse had used his influence to secure Rick's release, vouching for his good character and paying his bail money. Rick had been not only surprised but quite touched by the gesture.

In adversity people show their true colours, the young gynaecologist had thought to himself and Sir John Rawarse had come up trumps.

Rick had returned home to an initially hostile reception from his elderly next-door neighbour, until that is Enid discovered the truth. It wasn't long before Enid was eating humble pie. For not only did the old lady discover that Rick was indeed a doctor, but also that he had been telling her the truth when he 'borrowed' her car. His own car had truly been stolen and he had needed to get to the hospital in an emergency. Even worse for Enid, was that to her horror she had discovered that the young life he had saved that night, had been that of her very own niece, a Miss Belinda Jones. With the truth out, Enid had become contrite, dropped all charges and following Rick's release from the police cells, she had appeared at his front door with a homemade Steak and Kidney pie and a sincere apology. Even her previously hostile little mutt, Molly, had come around and the ferocious snarl had been replaced with a wagging tail and adoring eyes. Following this life-saving episode, Rick could do no wrong in the old lady's eyes. She became his champion and the two of them became good friends.

But there had been a complication to all this. Rick had fallen for the favourite niece, Belinda Jones, the young woman whose life he had saved, and feelings had been reciprocated. Following her discharge from hospital, the two of them had started dating, with the approval of Enid, but various hospital colleagues had warned Rick that it was unethical to date patients that he had treated or cared for and in particular a patient whose life he had saved. Doubts had started to cloud Rick's mind, and these drove a wedge between the two of them. They had had endless discussions about what they should do. Rick suggested that perhaps it would be wisest to leave things for a while and if they still felt the same for each other in a year or so – then perhaps they would get back together. Rick had been relieved that he hadn't slept with her – it would have made things so much more complicated. They parted on amicable terms, although Belinda had stated there would never be anyone else for her – she understood his inner conflict and after all was happy just to be alive. And so Rick found himself single again, but not without many female admirers.

Rick shifted slightly in the warm water of his luxurious bath, lifted his foot and turned on the hot tap. He was certainly enjoying some 'Me' time, and lay there in absolute ecstasy, complete with rubber duck bobbing in the bubbles. It had been an eventful year for Rick. As well as the ups and downs with Belinda and of course Enid, he had been delighted with his recent appointment to consultant obstetrician and gynaecologist in his favourite South Wales hospital. The work was varied, fulfilling and at times great fun, although there were inevitably times of sadness and loss, as would be expected. Following Rick's appointment, his previous consultant mentor and boss, Sir John Rawarse, had taken a well-deserved retirement and surprising everyone, he had moved to the Dordogne with a delightful young woman he met on the internet. This followed the tragic death of his beloved wife of 35 years and no one had ever dreamed that the old boy would find love again. But find love once more, he certainly did.

Sir John Rawarse had been a stalwart of the NHS, and had worked tirelessly to improve the wellbeing of his patients for three decades. The death of his wife and then his own unexpected cardiac arrest had clearly made him think twice about life and work. Given the choice between staying on at the NHS coalface, working himself to the death, or moving somewhere with good weather, good wine, in the company of a delightful young woman, he had decided on the latter. Rick had grown very fond of the old man as well as respecting him immensely and wished him well in his new life. But when Sir John had left, Rick had missed him more than expected and so was thrilled to receive a crate of wonderful red wines from 'Rawarse Vineyards', with the message:

Should have done this years ago. Life is brilliant.

Hope all is well with you and remember – Don't let the Bastards grind you down.

Regards, Sir John.

Rick had smiled as he read the message and could only imagine that his old boss, who had previously been rather pompous and frightening, had finally chilled out and was now thoroughly enjoying a new stab at life. He fondly remembered the old fellow, both his antics and his advice. Rick lifted his arm out of the warm suds of his bubble bath and raised his beer bottle. "Here's to you, sir, and bless you."

As well as Sir John Rawarse undergoing some pretty tumultuous changes in his life, there had also been some major upheavals in Rick's too. Rick's appointment to a consultant post brought with it new responsibilities and challenges for now the buck stopped with him! The care of any patient under his name was ultimately his responsibility, even if he himself had never seen the patient. He found himself becoming ever more vigilant and conscientious, which was good for the patients but took its toll on the young, new consultant. He also found himself becoming slightly frustrated at the slow-moving cogs of the NHS, in terms of trying to bring about positive change. There had already been many occasions when his proposals and ideas to improve patient care had been initially welcomed by management, talked about endlessly in multiple meetings, and then forgotten about until the next pointless meeting. Rick had given up on a number of his proposed improvement issues, not because he wasn't still passionate, but because he knew it was pointless. He now frequently skipped the ever increasing number of meetings to concentrate on seeing patients. He had established early on that he was a clinician not a politician.

Rick's watery contemplation was abruptly disturbed by the chimes of his doorbell. He ignored the intrusion, sunk further below the waterline and hoped for the best. But the chimes sounded again.

"Blast, bugger and damn!" he swore as he rose from his warm, watery haven. Bath water slapped over the side, taking with it the rubber duck. Rick cursed again; he picked up the duck from the pool of water on the floor, wrapped himself in a rather frayed old towel and stumbled down the stairs to the hall. Feeling thoroughly irritated, he flung open the front door.

"W-h-a-t!" he exclaimed in a manner that suggested he was mightily peeved. The early evening sun silhouetted a slim figure standing before him. He wasn't quite sure who it was at first, but then realisation dawned and as soon as he knew who it was that was standing at his front door, he wished he hadn't opened the damn thing. There he stood, hair wet and still covered in bubbles, his bare chest dripping water onto the ornate tiled hall floor and a gawping open mouth. He had a rubber duck in one hand, with the other clutching the towel that only just concealed his crown jewels. Rick looked like a right numpty.

Standing sedately at his front door, looking absolutely stunning was no less than Sister Alicia Granger.

"Um, sorry to have disturbed you… um… and your duck." She supressed a chuckle before continuing, "I thought that I would just introduce myself. I am your new next-door neighbour, oh, and so sorry for any inconvenience, you know the removal van and stuff. By the way, my name is Alicia."

"Oh, um, very nice to meet you Alicia," Rick stumbled over this words, "and um, welcome to the street." He felt such an idiot. He stepped backwards away from the threshold of the little house's entrance, tripping over a pair of abandoned shoes as he did so, and his towel started to slip. He dropped the rubber duck whilst grabbing the end of the towel in an attempt to preserve his modesty. Alicia couldn't help herself, she started to laugh.

"I am so sorry, it is obviously not a good time, but I am sure I will see you around – sorry to have caught you at a bad time. I hope you and the um… duck enjoy the rest of your bath." With that she turned with a huge smile on her face, walked the few steps to the front gate and was gone.

As Rick closed the front door, he cursed. When he had recently witnessed Alicia Granger standing up to Mr Henry Horsham on the surgical ward he had been mightily impressed. She was competent, well liked, and good looking. And from what he could tell she also had a good heart. For her to have seen him like this was grossly unfair. Please God she had not recognised him – if she had, surely any potential good impressions were now trashed.

"Ah well, another one bites the dust," he moaned as he trudged back up the stairs to finish his ablutions.

Alicia chuckled to herself as she carefully closed Rick's front gate, walked the few steps to her own front door and entered her new home. She could have sworn she knew her new next-door neighbour, but couldn't quite put her finger on it. However, it had occurred to her that whoever he was, he wasn't bad looking and had a physique that wasn't too shabby. Perhaps it was fate that she had moved here and met her next door neighbour with nothing but a towel wrapped around him and a rubber duck in his hand.

"I wonder, but then again he's probably got a long-term girlfriend or is gay... Ah well, c'est la vie," she whispered to herself and then turned her attention to her new home. She was so very excited. This was her first ever house and she already loved it, although it needed a fair amount of work and everything was dated. *Lick of paint here and there and it'll be good as new,* Alicia thought and then busied herself unpacking some of her boxes.

CHAPTER 4

The following day, Rick was in work bright and early.
Usually his team of junior doctors including a
registrar and senior house officer, would join him on
his early morning ward round, but not today, as
apparently they had been called away to see a patient
in A&E . When he arrived on the Delivery Suite, he
was joined by the lead midwife, and the anaesthetic
team to do a 'board' round. Each patient had their
name, past medical history, and if in labour, progress,
meticulously written on a white board in the staff
room. The team methodically went through the
details of each patient. That morning there were two
elective caesarean sections to be done, two women in
labour, one of whom was struggling and finally a
patient who to her credit had just delivered an eleven
pound baby boy. She had been in labour for nearly
twenty four hours, was exhausted and now the

midwife in charge had been alerted to the fact that she was bleeding heavily.

The lady in question was Rick's immediate priority and as he quickly walked towards her delivery room at the opposite end of labour ward, he thought to himself, 'Ouch, eleven pounds! That's a toddler not a baby, poor darling. Please God may her bleeding be settling'. It was known that the longer the labour and the bigger the baby, the greater the risk of subsequent bleeding. Sometimes litres of the red stuff were lost and Rick was all too aware, that postpartum haemorrhage was one of the most common causes of maternal death.

Rick broke out into a cold sweat and could feel his heart pounding when he arrived outside the labour room accompanied by the ward sister and a grumpy anaesthetist called Eric. Immediately adjacent to the newly-delivered mother's room, was a trolley with soiled sanitary pads and towels soaked in blood….evidence that she had significantly bled. The concern on the faces of each member of the team was evident and Rick felt irritated that he had not been informed earlier. In emergencies such as this, minutes mattered and turning the situation around was made so much harder the longer treatment was withheld.

A young nursing assistant leisurely emerged from the room blocking Rick's entrance. She looked cool, calm and collected, not the usual frantic looking, face screwed up with anxiety scenario that generally greeted Rick on such occasions.

"Forgive me, but what the hell is going on?" Rick asked.

"Oh, Mr Donovan, good morning. Um...she has had a bit of a bleed. We called the registrar........she hasn't arrived yet, apparently she is in A&E, so Jesus came to our rescue. He is in there with her and everything seems to have settled."

Rick thought to himself, 'as long as he isn't giving her the last bloody rites' and then addressing the nursing assistant asked, "I beg your pardon?"

"Jesus is in there with the patient and I am sure she will be fine," the nursing assistant calmly responded.

Rick stood there dumbfounded. He wasn't quite sure if there had been an outbreak of religious fervour on the labour ward or if this woman had just come out of a fruit farm. But what he did know was that if one of his patients was having a massive postpartum haemorrhage he needed to be in there.

The labour ward sister smiled oddly to herself and looking at Rick, whispered, "Jesus has been known to perform miracles you know – he is an excellent male midwife."

By now Rick had had enough, either the whole sodding world was going mad, or he was delusional. He turned to the nursing assistant and said in a slightly raised voice, "If Jesus is in there with her, I am sure she is absolutely fine, but forgive me I need to just check myself."

With that Rick knocked on the delivery room door and entered without waiting for an answer. He was completely taken aback. Far from the expected chaotic blood bath, the atmosphere was serene with soft music playing and lights dimmed. By the patient's bed stood a bearded man in hospital blues smiling down at mother and her new born baby. The new mother looked radiant and certainly not at death's door.

The bearded man looked up, "Hello Mr Donovan, my name is Jesus. I am one of the new midwives. This is Sheila who unfortunately has had a bit of a loss, about 700ml, but nothing that a touch of *Syntocinon* and a good uterine massage couldn't sort out. The uterus is now nicely contracted, her loss has completely settled. Oh…. and the placenta was complete, her observations are normal, and I've sent off some blood to be tested, just to be sure."

Sheila smiled serenely up at Rick to confirm what the new male midwife had said.

Rick was almost speechless, but he managed to splutter out the words, "Oh …um…right ….ahhh…thank you….. *Jesus*. I'll leave you to it then," Then turning to Sheila he uttered, "And Congratulations to you!"

With that Rick left the tranquil atmosphere of that delivery room with a huge smile on his face. "Funny old life," he whispered and then went off to continue the remainder of the ward round.

*

The next priority was a young woman called Mary who was struggling in labour. Rick knocked on the labour room door and waited respectfully for an affirmative to come in. The midwife opened the door and bade him to enter. Rick smiled and quickly introduced himself to Mary and to her Mum who was standing by her side, looking more than a bit anxious. Mary had been labouring for nearly twelve hours already and she looked exhausted. Rick was informed that she was now fully dilated and pushing, but there hadn't been any progress in the last hour. He took a look at the baby's heart beat monitor and it showed that her baby was starting to get distressed, for every time Mary had a contraction, the baby's heart slowed right down, and was now staying down even when her contraction had finished. It was a sure sign that her unborn baby was stressed. The Medic asked for a pair of gloves and sought the patient's permission to examine her. Rick could see the concern etched on the face of her mother, and he recognised her look of helplessness. The midwife too was by now twitched and the anxiety in the room was palpable. Mary's screams signalled the start of another contraction, and her mother squeezed her hand. Mary never saw the single tear that trickled down her mother's cheek, for she was now oblivious to all and everything except the pain in her pelvis and the worry for her unborn child.

The midwife grabbed Mary's other hand and exclaimed, "Come on my love, use all your energy to push this baby out, you are nearly there. Chin on chest and PUSH!"

Mary obliged and with that the baby's heart rate dived again and now to a dangerously low level. Rick decided enough was enough, "Mary, forgive me but I need to do an internal on you. I need to examine you to see how we are going to deliver this baby of yours, is that OK?" he gently asked.

With her contraction fading, the young woman,

her face drenched in sweat looked desperately at Rick and then at the heart-monitoring machine adjacent to the delivery bed. Her baby's heart rate dropped yet again. The vulnerable young woman nodded her permission, but her eyes were now full of tears and dread. As Rick donned a pair of gloves and quickly examined her, another forceful contraction came. She screamed and writhing around unwittingly kicked out as Rick examined her. The Medic skilfully avoided her thrashing limbs, ducking a flying foot as he did so. He briefly remembered sustaining an impressive black eye from a previous similar encounter and was determined not to experience a repeat.

He turned urgently to the midwife. "Sister, I need her legs in stirrups with perhaps some gentle straps, some local anaesthetic, and a pair of forceps…. quickly please….oh and please call the paediatricians."

Letting go of Mary's hand, the midwife duly obliged and then to her credit asked, "Mr Donovan, what about an anaesthetist, should I call Eric?"

But by now it was too late for an epidural, so Rick declined. He would just have to use a local anaesthetic block himself. Rick looked again at the baby's heart monitor, he knew that he didn't have much time. He looked directly into his patient's eyes and calmly spoke, "Mary, I promise you that your baby is going to be fine, but I need you to trust me and I need you to help me. I am going to put some local anaesthetic in down below and then deliver your baby with some forceps. I will gently pull and I need you to push with all your might during your next contraction, is that OK?"

The young woman nodded her consent, in truth she didn't really have much choice, but she was reassured by Rick's gentle and confident manner, as well as his calm explanation. Her legs were gently placed in stirrups before she grabbed the midwife's hand again. Rick gowned up and sat between her legs before skilfully injecting local anaesthetic into her nether regions. He waited a few moments then applied the metal forceps to the unborn baby's head and waited for a contraction. Mary looked pleading at her own mother, who by now had turned rather pale. The young mother-to-be then nervously turned and looked pleadingly at the midwife before her eyes finally settled on the consultant obstetrician seated in front of her. The wait for the next contraction was excruciating.

As if there was not enough to contend with in that small delivery room, near disaster then struck. The sight of blood and amniotic fluid cascading from her daughter's nether regions was one thing to cope with, but the introduction of an enormous pair of spoons into her reclining daughter's fanny, was the trigger for Mary's mother to experience an induced episode of light headedness. She swayed precariously backwards and forwards for a few seconds before collapsing in a direct trajectory into Rick's lap.

Rick was not having a good morning. He managed an inaudible, "Oh Bollocks", and keeping one hand protectively holding the gently placed pair of forceps, he caught Mary's Mother with his other free hand and arm. Catastrophe was avoided in terms of a potential nasty head injury, but Rick's ability to concentrate on the task in hand was compromised by a semi-conscious woman rather to close for comfort and nestling into his lap.

Looking at the midwife, Rick pleaded, "Please Sister, for God's sake get some friggin' help".

But Mary wouldn't let go of the midwife's hand and before they both knew it, the next contraction had arrived and the baby's heart rate dropped like a stone. The young patient oblivious to her mother's less than ideal state, screamed in pain and started to push involuntarily.

Fortunately for all, the paediatricians who had

been called earlier arrived and sensibly removed Mary's mother from Rick's lap and ensured her wellbeing, allowing Rick to concentrate on the job in hand.

Together, medic and midwife encouraged the young woman to push with all her strength and resolve, and although the responsibility for the life and wellbeing of these two persons in their care was sometimes overwhelming, they both remained determined and calm. Rick applied firm traction on the forceps and with considerable relief noted the top of little one's head appear. He gently uncoupled the forceps, then taking a pair of scissors, Rick purposefully and competently cut Mary to avoid uncontrolled tearing. With one more supreme effort, a beautiful baby girl was born and delivered onto Mary's tummy. Rick could feel his own heart racing with anxiety and sweat soaked his theatre blues.

There was no initial sign of life as Rick efficiently clamped and cut the cord and then hurriedly passed the new-born to the waiting paediatric team. Time seemed to stop. Everyone in the room held their breath and all of them had pounding hearts, especially Mr Rick Donovan. As the paediatricians started to resuscitate Mary's baby, the silence in the room was almost unbearable. It was intermittently broken by a new mother's hushed sobs and the sound of the baby doctors whispering to each other in conspiratorial tones as they worked.

Yet still the silence persisted. Mary's mother had by now regained consciousness, and sat feeling foolish at her fainting episode and helpless for her daughter. She held Mary tightly and she too wept, but silently for her daughter's sake. Rick had bowed his head in quiet resignation, and then it happened. A muffled yelp, a whimper and then a beautiful, wonderful, full bellied cry. Rick looked up at the young woman who was his charge and smiled. And she smiled back at him through tears cascading down her wet cheeks. There was a "Wooppee!" and "Thank God for that," from the baby's proud mum and granny, and yet more tears flowed. The relief in the delivery room was palpable and most welcome. The paediatricians brought the baby back to his mother, and her midwife helped Mary to apply the infant to her breast. Mary hardly noticed Rick delivering her placenta and then stitch her up so that you would hardly have known she'd just given birth. An exhausted and emotionally drained Rick got up from his stool between Mary's legs, removed his soiled over gown, and washed his hands. As he walked out he looked back at the new mother with her cradled infant and doting grandmother.

"Congratulations all," he quietly voiced, but the small family were just at that moment too wrapped up in their own joy to see or acknowledge him. He left the room and continued the ward round.

By now the other labouring woman had delivered successfully and so Rick went to see the patients for elective caesarean section. He ensured their consents were in order and answered any outstanding questions that they had before returning to the changing room, showering and then putting on a fresh pair of hospital blues. The caesarean sections both went without a hitch and by the end of the morning, five beautiful bouncing babies had been safely delivered.

*

Sister Alicia Granger had arrived promptly at 0700hours on Bedlam ward to start her 12 hour shift. She was tired out on account of being up until 0100am moving furniture around her new house and deciding in which room she was going to start her epic decorating spree. Firstly, she attended handover of the patients on her ward from the night shift, writing down their details, why they had been admitted and their progress both from a medical and social perspective. When handover was complete, she organised and directed her staff to their respective tasks before walking around the ward to ensure everything was in order, from clean toilets to properly filled-out observation charts at the foot of each patient's bed. She had a kindly brief word with everyone she came across, smiling as she did so. She then returned to the ward reception where Phyllis was busy ensuring the notes for each consultant's ward round were ready and correct.

"Good morning Phyllis, are you OK this morning?" Alicia smiled.

"Good morning Sister, yes not bad thank you. Still got a pulse, which I suppose is a lot to be grateful for really." Phyllis grinned, her face beaming at the new ward sister and her latest ally. "How's your new house? You moved in yesterday didn't you?"

"Oh, it's fantastic….so exciting moving into my first proper house. I was up late arranging furniture and deciding where to make a start with the decorating."

"You should have a painting party. Anyhow have you met the neighbours yet?" Phyllis enquired.

"Matter of fact I did. On one side an old married couple, they must be in their 80s. I think she's got dementia, but he's a spritely old chap. They asked me in for a cup of tea and piece of cake to welcome me to the street. They told me all about the old lady I bought the house from, who by the sounds of it was a bit of a religious nutter. There were apparently regular prayer meetings in my house that often ended in a good fist fight!"

"Bloody hell, sounds fun. Did they get things going with some holy wine?" Phyllis chuckled.

"I don't know, but the old couple asked me if I was going to have any prayer meetings in my front room, and if I was, please could I keep them quiet. Then they got out the sweet sherry and it wasn't long before the two of them were sozzled. After polishing off the sherry, the old fella got out a bottle of Port! Anyhow, after that I quickly made my excuses... but still what a lovely old couple!"

Phyllis laughed, "What about the neighbours on the other side?"

"Well, the most bizarre thing. I rang on the doorbell, and then I heard this stomping down the stairs, with what sounded like someone swearing under their breath. The front door opened, and this bloke, dripping wet with a towel wrapped around him and a rubber duck in one hand, stood there gazing at me. I introduced myself, you know, "Hello, I am

Alicia, your new next door neighbour," and he looked all embarrassed, which I suppose given the circumstances was understandable. But then he replied in this rather posh accent, 'Oh, hello Alicia, welcome to the street." Then he started to back up, I suppose he felt a bit exposed, fell over a pair of shoes in his hall and damn near lost his towel!"

"Crickey, lost his towel as in the 'Full Monty? A pleasing sight?" Phyllis teased.

"No Phyllis," Alicia blushed. But then in a quieter almost conspiring tone added, "But from what I could see, nothing too disagreeable!" She smiled and raised an eyebrow.

They both laughed out loud and other staff on the ward turned to see the reason for the mirth, but the two of them disguised it well.

"You know Phyllis, the odd thing was that I recognised him from somewhere but I'm just not sure where." Alicia looked wistful.

The banter came to an abrupt end when true to form and completely on time, Mr Henry Horsham arrived with his team to do their morning ward round.

"Good morning Sister! Good morning Miss Jones!" Horsham bellowed.

"A very good morning to you too, Mr Horsham," Phyllis slowly replied with her most ingratiating smile, with just a hint of irreverence that poked a tiny bit of fun at the senior consultant.

"Ah…yes…well…ah..." Horsham spluttered, then recovering, "can we do the ward round please Sister?"

"Certainly, Mr Horsham," Alicia graciously answered, although she was laughing inside at his obvious boy like reaction to Phyllis's seductive look and micky taking.

The notes were neatly stacked in order, according to the position of the patients on the ward. They were taken up by the junior doctors and the ward round started. Again, Horsham was impressed by the thoroughness and knowledge of the young ward sister. Patients were reviewed, examined and plans were made in a safe, methodical and caring manner. Horsham almost relaxed in the knowledge that his patients were being well looked after and in comparison to his first meeting with Sister Alicia Granger, he actually started to ask her opinion on various matters of care.

"Thank you Sister, anyone else that I need to see?" Horsham asked.

"Well actually Mr Horsham, there is just one other

patient." Alicia responded. "You may remember you saw him in clinic last week. He was having problems with change in bowel habit, weight loss and excessive flatulence. I believe you wanted to investigate him by looking into his bowel with a scope to ensure no lesions in his rectum."

"Ah yes, I remember the chap. There were no spaces left in day care surgery so I thought we could just have a preliminary look to make sure there is no lesion." Horsham nodded. By that everyone knew he meant cancer.

This had become a regular feature of hospital work – the fitting in of patients to extra ad hoc appointments because of the lack of available clinic slots, and all credit to Mr Henry Horsham who could easily have just let the poor man wait the many weeks before a suitable appointment came up. Instead, he like many other of his hospital consultant colleagues went the extra mile and fitted in patients whenever and wherever he could, even if it meant in his own time. Phyllis who was only too aware of this, since she was often the one who made appointments for patients following their hospitalisation, admired him for it.

"Very well, lead on Sister." Horsham barked.

Phyllis, who was in earshot of the group of

gathered medics, whispered under her breath, "Oh, he's so commanding," she looked on with a rather disturbing, adoring look.

"I beg your pardon, what did you say?" Horsham questioned with a raised eyebrow.

"Just marvellous!" Phyllis responded and then in full view of the whole team as she gave her best smile and then openly winked at the increasingly embarrassed Henry Horsham. A muffled bout of suppressed titters reverberated among Horsham's team of junior doctors. Horsham turned a shade of a bright red, he coughed and spluttered, "Come on….come on…work to be done, don't you know!" And although he pretended to ignore the unashamed flirting of the ward receptionist, he was actually deep down rather chuffed.

Alicia guided Horsham to the treatment room, a small clinical area just off the ward. An elderly gentleman lay on the treatment bed with his anxious looking wife sitting on a chair by his side.

"Good morning Sir, I am Mr Horsham, do you remember me from last week? I just wanted to have a little look up your bottom, just to make sure there is no mischief there that would account for your bowel problems and weight loss. Is that OK?" Horsham smiled down at the old man paternalistically.

"Pardon me Mr Horsham, you'll have to forgive me, I am very deaf," the old man responded slowly and in monotone.

"I WILL NEED TO LOOK UP YOUR BOTTOM, IS THAT OK?" Horsham bellowed.

"I am so sorry, what did you say?" the old man spluttered.

"He wants to look up your bum Malcolm!" The patient's wife waded in, shrieking at the top of her voice into her husband's ear. "You know because you keep getting the shits," she added as a succinct way of explanation.

"Did you say Mr Horsham's got the shits? Why in God's name do I need to know that?" The old man screamed.

"No you deaf old sod, he hasn't got the shits, we need to look up YOUR bum, not his!" His long suffering and exasperated wife tried to explain.

The whole debacle proceeded for a further full hour before Malcolm had finally grasped the situation and consented to the procedure. By the time the old fellow had undergone a simple proctoscopy, Mr Henry Horsham was left in no doubt that his patient had a problem with diarrhoea. On opening the device to view his back passage, the brown stuff, together with a significant down flow of flatulence was released with such ferocity that it covered the unsuspecting consultant colorectal surgeon, requiring a shower and a full change of clothing.

Henry Horsham was not amused. Yet another humiliation, although afterwards they did all laugh, including the man himself. But the incident proved to them all, the point that every patient is a human being with different needs and requirements. A single patient may take many hours to sort out, and the managerial hierarchy often failed to appreciate such variations when deciding set numbers for their medical colleagues to see, diagnose and treat.

That day Phyllis Jones fell in love with Henry Horsham. On hearing that despite being covered in shit, he maintained a professional yet caring attitude to the old man and his wife, she made it her mission to seduce him. Sister Alicia Granger was also impressed and had seen a new side to her consultant colleague. She knew that if she worked hard and cared properly for the patients, she would always have his support.

The rest of the day on Bedlam ward proceeded without a hitch. It was late afternoon when Rick

Donovan arrived to do a ward round on his gynaecology patients. His registrar had already been around after sorting out a patient in A&E, but Rick liked to double check everything was in order. He had purposefully left it late in the day in order to avoid the ward sister who was now his new next door neighbour. After their unexpected liaison the evening before when Rick had felt a bit of an idiot, he wanted to leave it a good few days before seeing her again. On entering the ward, Phyllis looked up from the reception desk and pleasantly greeted him, before busying herself obtaining the patient notes for his ward round. The duty staff nurse accompanied him and he methodically carried out his work reviewing each of his patients and ensuring all was well with their management. When he had finished, Rick thanked the staff nurse who had accompanied him, and on his way out of the ward gave a cheery smile to Phyllis.

He thought he'd got away with it and breathed a sigh of relief, but on walking down the corridor back to the main hospital thoroughfare, there she was. A group of nursing colleagues were strolling back to Bedlam after taking a break and Alicia Granger was with them. They were laughing and joking animatedly as they approached and it was evident they were good friends and colleagues. As Rick walked up to them, he bade them a 'good afternoon' as was appropriate and tried to hurry on by. The nurses looked up, smiled and returned his greeting, continuing to chat as they strolled by. All accept Sister Alicia Granger. She stopped in her tracks and quizzically looked again at Rick. "I know him as Mr Donovan but there is more to it than that," she thought.

Then realisation struck. "Oh my God, he's my new next door neighbour. The guy in the towel with the rubber duck!" She wasn't sure if she thought it or said it, but Alicia's heart missed a beat. Her colleagues, who by now had walked further up the corridor, turned and called her to re-join them. The thing was, she was still just too shocked and then the devil in her came out. Alicia Granger just couldn't help herself. "Ah Mr Donovan, good to see you with your clothes on; incidentally how is the duck?"

Rick didn't know whether to laugh or to run. Initially his defences went up and ignoring her remark, he responded with a rather pompous, "Nice to see you too, Sister. I've seen my patients on Bedlam, there are a few actions that need to be addressed but I am sure that the staff nurse who accompanied me will keep you informed."

Alicia was disappointed with the reply, until Rick with a beaming smile and raised eyebrow added, "Oh and by the way, the duck is fine ......thank you." They both laughed and her smile was wonderful.

"Oh God, I think I'm falling in love," they both thought as they continued on their respective ways.

CHAPTER 5

The psychiatric ward was buzzing, literally. A middle aged, rather plain housewife had recently been admitted after her husband had buggered off with the au pair. She had subsequently taken to smoking rather large quantities of a particularly powerful batch of pot, which it was thought provoked the development of a psychotic delusional state in which she thought she was a bee. The resultant buzzing noises of the woman as she 'flew' around the ward, slurping up any sugar from anywhere that it was available was literally driving the staff mad – particularly since the administered anti-psychotic drugs had been slow to make any significant difference to her mental state. Other patients complained about the constant buzzing, and took a dislike to the poor woman, particularly when she stuck her nose in their recently sugared tea and tried to snort it up. Dick Chambers on the other hand could well understand her fascination with flying even if it was in the guise of an insect and did his best to be nice to her. The human bee wasn't the only person Dick Chambers was nice to. The staff and patients alike soon realised that he was an extraordinarily decent chap. As he started to get better from his manic depression, his true nature was slowly evolving back to the lovely man that he was.

That is not to say that he still didn't have any hiccups with regard to his mental health. After being rescued from the seventh floor of the hospital building by an athletic gynaecologist, he knew that he was lucky to be alive and that realisation became ever more real to him as he started to recover. He felt that he must have been spared for some purpose. Every day he still thought about his beloved wife, Ann, and he still spoke to her, sitting in front of a photograph of her that he kept by his bedside cabinet. He told her about life on the ward, he told her that he missed her terribly, but that hopefully she was doing OK. When she spoke back to him, it was now a normal sane voice that he heard in his mind and heart. She told him to stop being sad for her, that she loved him more than anything or anyone that had ever lived, but that now he must enjoy the rest of his life and ensure that where he could, he should help others with their suffering. So slowly Dick Chamber's fascination with flying started to subside. Reality and stability returned to his once troubled mind and he started to get better. From time to time, the depressive mode of his illness would come to the fore and he would relapse with feelings of hopelessness and sadness. But then he would hear Ann's voice telling him to get on with it and be an agent for change and happiness in other people's lives, and he would strive once more to get well. No doubt it was the drugs that were helping him to recover, but also the kindness of the staff on the ward and his own outlook on life.

As his recovery continued, he became ever more conscious of a female patient who would sit in the far corner of the ward's communal sitting room. She always looked so sad, and frequently wept openly. On occasions, completely out of the blue, she would fly into an unprovoked rage and her left eyebrow would twitch madly. Then she would collapse, exhausted, her energy spent, and become quiet and contrite about her previous behaviour. It broke his heart to see her so unhappy and he made it his mission to bring some joy back into her life. Her name was Joyce Evans.

The inhabitants of the psychiatric ward were a mixed and necessarily crazy bunch. Psychotics, depressives, personality disorders, patients with mania, and more recently a schizophrenic patient called Roger who was also unlucky enough to be suffering with Tourette's syndrome. Roger would walk in circles in the main communal living area of the ward, swearing, twitching and 'ticcing'. The psychotic part of his illness had resurfaced when he had been placed back in the community and had literally been forgotten about. Unsurprisingly, he hadn't taken his medication and before long, he was as bad as ever. But unlike the vast majority of patients with Tourette's syndrome, Roger also had a nasty streak within him whether he was mentally well or had relapsed. He had a tendency to behaviour that was sexist, racist, and misogynistic all rolled up in a fascist outlook. This, mixed with his zealous lack of inhibitions proved a cocktail for potential disaster. And this cocktail had very nearly cost him his life on more than one occasion.

Just before his readmission, he had attended an extreme right-wing political gathering to feed his warped appetite for all things fascist. The meeting was held in a relatively small venue and Roger had found himself standing between two enormous tattooed skinheads, one of whom had an obvious lack of teeth, the assumption being that they had been knocked out during some form of violent episode. The get-together had started to get into full swing with clenched fists punching the air and the chanting of racist rhetoric. After a while the main speaker of this gruesome gathering, who was a little bespectacled man, dressed in a smart suit, quietened the small frenzied crowd down to ask for comments or feedback from those assembled in his midst. Any reflective and logical debate soon faltered and so the little white fascist resorted to the usual brain dead antics.

Addressing his fascist flock he shouted out, "Who are we? Who am I?"

The skinhead standing next to Roger bellowed out, "You are white, you are right, you rule!" The small gathering punched their fists into the air, echoing these words, "We are white, we are right, we rule!" before finally settling down once more. Roger followed suite and found he was really starting to enjoy himself. These were his sort of people.

Then the little bespectacled man, not content with the previous outbursts shouted out once again, "Who are we? Who am I?"

Roger could feel a tic coming and the toothless skinhead to his left looked quizzically down on him as he concentrated hard to subdue any sudden uncontrolled urges. But alas for Roger, any self-control was entirely lost. Without any warning his arm flew out sideways into the path of the enormous skinhead to the side of him as he shouted out into the crowd, "Bastards, F-ing bastards!" Those gathered looked around incredulously to see a diminutive Roger and the enormous assaulted skinhead with a bleeding nose. In disbelief they watched it happen again, the same arm movement but with a different vocal, "Tossers… F-ing tossers!" This time the skinhead sustained a black eye. It was to be Roger's final action and comment for the night since it was followed by a great deal of violence towards the unwitting critique of the far right and thereafter Roger was admitted to the hospital trauma unit. After sorting his broken arm, fractured jaw and multiple bruises, he was transferred onto the psychiatric wing, heartbroken that he had so offended his favourite bunch of people.

Roger's unkind nature continued to manifest itself after his admission to the psychiatric ward. He was horrible to anyone and everyone he came across, particularly if they were female, non-white and didn't adhere to his distorted view of the world. In addition, experience had taught him to concentrate his vile comments at those who were already vulnerable. Joyce Evans was one such soul. Somehow Roger had learnt that the precipitating factor for Joyce's ill health had been the death of her beloved dog, Geoffrey. This information had probably come to him from the misjudged whisperings of the nursing staff who he had overheard. He didn't know who had stolen Joyce's dog and then thrown him from the seventh floor of the hospital, but the fact that he knew the precipitating factor for her misery was enough and he would use such knowledge as a weapon!

One particular morning Joyce was sitting quietly by herself in the main sitting room. The sun was shining and its warm rays filtered through the large framed windows of the ward. She had progressed from a state of melancholic silence interspersed with bouts of gentle crying to actually acknowledging the presence of others, saying "Thank you", when a member of staff gave her a cup of tea or even attempting the odd smile when someone was kind to her. The general feeling among the medical staff was that she was making good progress. Some of the improvement in her mental state had been secondary to the thoughtful words and deeds of one particular inpatient, Dick Chambers. He was always so polite, well-mannered and caring of her. Although there was not a lot of verbal communication between them, a quiet trust was developing. This was helping not only Joyce to recover, but also Dick.

However, it had become one person's mission to upset this finely balanced recuperation and that person was the mean-spirited Roger. On one particular morning, when he came into the sitting room and saw Joyce sitting alone, he grabbed his chance for malice.

"Good morning Joyce." He ticced with a sudden jerk of his head as he spat out the words. "Nice morning for a dog walk, don't you think?" He smiled malevolently as she looked at him in disbelief. "Oh, I forgot your dog is dead, isn't he… and dead mongrels don't go for walkies, do they?" Roger laughed at his own cruelty. "Anyhow, now he's a dead dog, perhaps he is flying around in heaven… couldn't fly around on earth, could he… tried to fly from the top of the hospital… didn't do him much good, did it?" His arm flew out involuntarily as he ticced, "Bollocks, shit, bollocks!" The Tourette's worsened, the crueller he became.

A tear trickled down Joyce's cheek. She turned away from her persecutor and looked out of the window, hiding her hurt as best she could. Unbeknown to them both, Dick Chambers had come into the sitting room. He hadn't heard the entire episode of taunting, but he knew that Roger was being a cruel bastard.

"You say one more word, you son of a bitch, and

God help me I will punch the living daylights out of you!" Dick fumed; he had turned bright red and stood with his fists clenched.

"You and wh…..who…..whose army, you old git?" Roger spluttered the words out but was slightly disturbed by the ferocity of Dick's stance. Dick looked the younger man directly in the eyes and started to stride towards him.

As Dick approached him, Roger snarled, "Come on then you old sod and I'll kick your bloody teeth in!"

Dick remained silent and although he was almost twice the age of his disrespectful rival, Dick wasn't in the least bit intimidated. Roger waited, allowing Dick to get within striking distance and then without any warning took a pre-emptive strike at the older man. Roger's fist swiped the air completely failing to make contact. Dick, resorting back to his old military training, ducked under the flying knuckles and then straightening out landed a punch of his own into the younger man's mid-rift. It wasn't a killer blow, but enough to wind him and certainly one that would make the antagonist think twice before mocking Joyce again. Roger stumbled 'F-ing and Blinding' out of the room.

"You speak to her again like that and it won't be the psychiatric hospital you'll need, it'll be the trauma unit

AGAIN," Dick shouted after him. He took a deep breath to calm himself and then went over to where Joyce was sitting. He sat beside her and taking his handkerchief out of his pocket, proceeded to gently wipe away her tears. Then the two of them just sat in silence looking out of the window at a glorious sunny morning. Then an extraordinary and wonderful thing happened. The 55-year-old spinster who had always been too proper, too religious, and too correct to even entertain the idea of a having a man in her life, reached out and took Dick's hand. A simple, "Thank you," with a slight squeeze of his hand was all that she could manage, but it was enough, and heralded the real start of the rehabilitation of them both.

Days passed into weeks and a general harmonious atmosphere pervaded the psyche ward. Patients seemed to get better, for the moment at least, and many were discharged back into the community, with their acute mental illnesses healed. Even the 'human bee' had stopped buzzing around the ward and there had been no further trouble from Roger who seemed to have quietened down considerably. The relationship between Dick and Joyce had blossomed into something rather special. They would sit for hours in each other's company, sometimes in silence, sometimes talking about the world and its problems and occasionally about their respective past lives. Joyce learnt of Dick's deceased wife, his subsequent sorrow and descent into mental illness, but she never ascertained the details of his manic state and the fact that her new best friend was indeed the one responsible for the death of her beloved dog. In his quieter moments of the day, Dick would seek the solace of his own side room and once in the privacy afforded by a closed door, he would whisper to his beloved Ann and ask her if she minded him becoming ever closer to Joyce. The answer he received was always a categorical 'no', she only wanted him to be happy and to get on with the remainder of his life. And so the friendship between Dick and Joyce became ever closer, but as the weeks passed by he was yet to see her laugh; the occasional smile but never an unguarded wholesome laugh. One particular afternoon that was all to change – not only would he see her laugh, but he would get a glimpse of her true metal.

The staff of the psychiatric unit had all been preparing for an important visit from the new Minister of Health, the newly knighted 'Sir' Archibald Harrington-Smythe. The new knight of the realm had previously been a Chief Executive of the same hospital Health Board and in government circles at least he was thought to be 'returning home'. In fact during his time as the previous Chief Exec, 'Sir' Archibald had presided over one of the worst times in the Health Board's history and locally was remembered for being ineffectual and incompetent. In short he had been a complete plonker and had been respected as much as the local cat's arse. Apparently, the current Chief Executive, a Mrs Marjory Manson had begrudgingly agreed to accompany the ministerial entourage after considerable pressure from central government. The tour of the hospital facilities was to be recorded for local television, and the press had been invited by the vain Minister in the hope of a propaganda triumph depicting him as a caring, as well as competent member of the cabinet.

The psychiatric unit and its wards had been cleaned, brushed and polished, and a VIP coffee morning with appropriate condiments had been prepared in the ward day room. Any potential violent or abusive patients had been banged up or removed from the proposed route of the exclusive party, to ensure no verbal or physical mishaps could cause possible offence. The patients themselves were told to be on their best behaviour and were warned of the consequences of inappropriate remarks or conduct.

Having completed their tour of the medical and

surgical facilities, the ministerial troupe arrived dead on time at the psychiatric ward, surrounded by a troupe of flashing cameras and open microphones. The Minister stood tall and rather toffee-nosed, with an arrogant air of one who was more worried about his own self-importance and progression than he ever was with the wellbeing of other individuals or indeed patients, unless of course it was going to win him votes. Despite being in charge of the whole show, he was still a man who had absolutely no idea of the working conditions of staff or the suffering of patients, and worst still he really didn't care. When Sir Archibald walked into the unit and greeted the staff, he did so with a lofty conceit and condescending manner. Both the staff and patients felt looked down upon, and most saw through his false small talk and feigned concern.

Contrary to this man's self-importance, Marjory Manson, the accompanying Chief Executive was a down-to-earth, see-as-you-speak, good-hearted individual. More importantly she really did have her patients' best interests at heart. She secretly disapproved of the Minister who was her guest, but for the sake of political correctness she tolerated him and maintained a decorum of civility, through a gritted smile.

As the VIPs arrived at the Psychiatric Unit with

their entourage, they filed into the main communal sitting area where Dick, Joyce and a few other patients were sitting and quietly chatting away to each other. However, one significant mistake the lead psychiatric nurse had made was not to ensure the absolute exclusion of Roger from the vicinity. Although he was barred from the communal sitting area for the visit, he had surreptitiously sneaked in. The Minister had been given a cup of tea and an iced bun and was busy persuading one of the inpatients of the quality of the Psychiatric Unit and so by association was blowing his own trumpet.

"What a nice unit you have here. I, of course, facilitated the upgrade you know. What do you think of that?" Harrington-Smythe asked in a rather loud and overbearing pompous voice.

"It's shit." The word came out of nowhere and the room was suddenly hushed.

"I beg your pardon?" The Minister's complexion became beetroot red, and he turned to face his critic.

"It's shit….. and you are a wanker!" The words seemed to repeat themselves, but it was difficult to make out where they came from and just who the offender was. The TV cameras were rolling and the journalists present, sensing a story, pricked up their ears and started scribbling away in their notebooks.

"How dare you speak to me like that! Don't you know who I am?"

Titters had started going around the room and the Chief Executive, fearing a diplomatic disaster, entered into the fray.

"Sir Archibald, please pay no attention, the words are not directed at you; some of our patients do have disinhibition problems and involuntary swearing can be a problem. It is just the illness." The Chief Executive was wonderfully diplomatic. The journalists all looked slightly disappointed and then again from the back of the room it came again.

"Archibald is a tosspot, a big, fat wanker."

The room erupted into a frenzy of laughter. Joyce who from her days working on the surgical wards had intensely disliked the man, laughed openly and Dick thought it was wonderful. She then did the most unexpected and brave thing. She stood up from the sofa and walked over to where Sir Archibald stood and with the cameras rolling started to softly speak.

"You sir, are a fake and a cad. You care only about your own position and self-importance. Worse still, is the false sincerity and pretence that you care about our NHS." Sighing, Joyce added, "Shame on you.

And whoever said that rude word about you is absolutely correct."

All hell broke loose and to make matters worse on the diplomatic front, Roger, who had been responsible for the outbursts was emboldened by Joyce's words and flung himself forward from the back of the room. "Archie is an F-ing twat, do da, do da," and as he came forward singing at the top of his voice, he twitched, his flailing right arm and fist connected with the Minister's scone and cream and then the politician's nose.

This was the final insult for Sir Archibald Harrington-Smythe. He simply lost it. It was now difficult to tell the difference between the mentally ill and the Government Minister. In fact any outsider looking in would have sworn that Sir Archibald Harrington-Smythe was the nutter among the collected ensemble. He was seething with rage at this most public display of civil disobedience and lack of respect. He took a lunge at Roger, flooring him in the process, and then unbelievably turning to Joyce swung at her too.

It was Mrs Marjory Manson who stopped the Minister's arm reaching its target. The Chief Executive's self-defence classes had finally paid off, although Marjory herself later regretted the utterance that went with it. The words, "Don't you touch her, you bloody bastard," seemed a somewhat inappropriate remark to make for the Chief Executive of a major Health Board to the United Kingdom's Minister for Health. When Sir Archibald tried the same feat with his other fist, it was Dick Chambers who reacted like lightning. He was up off the sofa in a flash and it was his boot's contact with the self-important man's goolies that stopped the Minister dead in his tracts. As Sir Archibald crumpled to the ground, clutching his by now rather tender testicles, a round of applause went around the room for both a respected Chief Executive and indeed for a psychiatric inpatient named Dick Chambers.

Joyce, who had witnessed again Dick's unquestioning defence of her, took his trembling hands in her own and looking at him directly in the eyes, reached up and kissed him full on the mouth. It was a wonderful shock for the two of them and Dick with the blessing of his deceased wife, took her in his arms and held her, closely and lovingly.

Needless to say the incident hit the national and local newspapers the following day and was reported on national and international television that same evening. Sir Archibald Harrington-Smythe was dismissed from the cabinet in disgrace and was replaced by a more suitable Minister. One with common sense and an appreciation of humility. Praise was heaped on Mrs Marjory Manson for her cool head and the defence of her patients. Her position as chief executive was strengthened, as was her ability to secure much needed funds for the Health Board from central Government. The papers described Roger, Dick and Joyce and the part they played in the Minister's downfall from grace. One particular journalist who had really done his homework described the relationship each had with the other, and part of his column, together with a photograph of Dick and Joyce embracing, read:

It is gratifying to see the effects of patient power in the dismantling of an unsuitable character from government office, particularly when that individual had in the opinion of many respectable health experts, presided over a number of ill-conceived policies to the detriment of our NHS. It is also interesting to note the wonder of forgiveness among the general public and how out of disaster new relationships can flourish. Ms Joyce Evans was the lady who voiced the opinion of the nation when she agreed with words of one of her fellow inpatients, that Sir Harrington-Smythe was 'a big fat wanker'. Harrington-Smythe was then prevented from assaulting the good lady by a combination of quick thinking and fast reflexes, courtesy of the chief executive and indeed an inpatient by the name of Mr Dick Chambers, an ex-RAF pilot. The photograph depicts Ms Evans with the Mr Chambers who defended her so admirably. The embrace you see certainly gives the impression of a wonderful friendship and perhaps more. Love can occur anywhere, at any time, even on a psychiatric ward and even in the presence of past hurts. I have a reliable source who informs me that it was the very man who Ms Evans is seen embracing following the fracas, who indeed was responsible for her current ill health and admission. For it was Mr Dick Chambers who was instrumental in the death of her much loved dog some months ago, the grief of which precipitated her pathological psychological state. Yet we see reconciliation at its best and perhaps even the blossoming of new love. Some would argue the Minister's visit although unfortunate, was successful in all sorts of unforeseen ways.

*

The morning after the Health Minister's visit, Joyce sat in her place on the sofa by the window overlooking the hospital gardens and reading the newspaper. Dick was sitting next to her doing a crossword. He looked across at his newfound soulmate and smiled at her. She looked up from the paper, her eyes brimming with tears.

"It was you… you who killed my Geoffrey."

CHAPTER 6

It was dark and cold when Rick finally arrived home. It had been another long and exhausting day at the hospital coalface. He had been in the operating theatre for the whole of that afternoon doing a hysterectomy on a woman with the most severe pelvic disease he had ever seen. The unfortunate patient's womb had been plastered to her bowel and rectum and Rick had had to ask for the help of one of his surgical colleagues who specialised in bowel surgery.

Mr Henry Horsham had been on call and so came to the gynaecologist's operating theatre to assist. Together, the two of them had worked for many hours stooped over the unfortunate woman's open abdomen to successfully complete an extremely difficult operation, and Rick could quite happily say that he was knackered. Henry Horsham had been an absolute star and Rick had thanked him profusely before writing up his operation notes and making his way home. As a consultant gynaecological surgeon, Rick never really left his work at the hospital, like most consultants he would carry various patients around in his thoughts. Even if it was subconscious, he would be working out ways to deal with their problems or worrying about their postoperative wellbeing.

His home was his refuge. He would collapse, crack open a beer, have a shower and then perhaps order a takeaway if he couldn't be bothered to cook, which was more often than not these days. Sometimes Rick would do some paperwork that he hadn't managed to sort out during the day and then perhaps watch a movie before retiring to bed. Since he was surrounded by people all day at work, whether colleagues or patients, he valued his own time and space in the privacy of his own home, where he could just be himself. He knew he was hugely privileged to be party to some of the most intimate details of his patients' lives in his work as a doctor. There was plenty of meaning in his life and he felt himself fortunate to be able to help folk to the best of his ability. So overall, Rick Donovan felt fulfilled in both his work and social life, often going for a beer with colleagues and friends. Yet still something was missing. Tonight as he lounged on his sofa recovering from his traumatic day at the office, he felt a yearning for something more and as if on cue the front door bell rang.

"Oh bugger, no peace for the wicked," Rick initially protested as he got up from the sofa and walked to the front door. But when he saw who was standing there, he immediately relented.

"Alicia, hi! How nice to see you, come in please… can I get you a drink or something?" He mused that maybe he was just a little too enthusiastic, but needn't have worried when she beamed a wonderful smile at him and pulled out a bottle of red wine.

"Glass of red perhaps?" she enquired.

He laughed, "Fantastic, you read my mind. Come on in and take the weight off your pins. I'll get a couple of glasses." Rick was unashamedly delighted by the intrusion from his next-door neighbour and he poured them each a glass of Chardonnay and handed one to Alicia. "For you, madame," he gestured.

"I think you'll find that that it is 'mademoiselle', a madame in my book is a brothel owner!" Alicia raised her eyebrows and gave him a cheeky grin. They laughed.

"You may be many things Alicia, but one of them is not the keeper of a house of ill repute! Anyhow, it's great to see you, the duck and I have missed you."

"Well to be honest, I was half expecting a half-naked man with his best friend, but I guess you will just have to do." She chuckled and he contemplated how pretty she was. They sat on Rick's battered old sofa, relaxed into each other's company, glass of wine in hand, and started to freely chatter away.

"I don't know about you, but I have had the day from hell. That patient who had the hysterectomy today on my list... well, her operation was an absolute surgical nightmare with everything stuck to buggery, the poor love. I had to get one of the bowel boys to give me a hand. Henry Horsham pitched up and you know what... he was fabulous. Still took us the best part of three hours, instead of the usual 45 minutes." Rick sighed.

"Is she OK now?" The concern on Alicia's face was very real.

"Oh yes, she'll be fine now, but no wonder she had so much pain beforehand," Rick responded.

"Well, if it is any consolation, I had a bloody awful day too."

"Why?" Rick raised an eyebrow.

"Well we had finished the rounds and then I had to sort out dear old Mrs Taylor, a new admission from that useless new care home. She is not one of your patients, Rick, but poor love is doubly incontinent, demented, just about walks with a Zimmer, and let me tell you she is very stubborn. Anyhow, she comes in from her residential home... How can I say this nicely...? Soiled is probably the best way to describe her, but it is everywhere. Honestly my heart went out to her. How anyone can let another human being get into that state, I don't know. So, we get her stripped off and clean her up as best we can. Then I need the hoist to get her into the bath. Well you guessed it, love her, once in the bath she decides to loosen her bowels once again and these turds are floating around, so definitely time to get her out. But then the bloody hoist breaks down and to make matters infinitely worse, Mrs Taylor is about the size of a small elephant."

"Oh my god, here, have a top-up. I think I know what is coming." Rick filled her glass with some more of the red stuff.

"So now yours truly is in the bottom end of the bath, forgive the pun, you know the one with floating turds in it. We have three other members of staff trying to lift her out and eventually have to call Bob the porter because we just cannot shift her. To cut a long story short... poor old Bob, who I have to say was a bit reluctant to say the least; well, he was magnificent and thank God for his strength. But finally there she is back in the chair, covered up and clean. Bob, bless him, is now in a bit of a state – he smelt of poo, since he had had to get in the bath to hoist the old girl out, and subsequently knackered his back. Anyhow, despite it all, he then turned to Mrs Taylor to ask if she is OK. Her response? She turned, faced him and then screamed at him, calling him 'a bloody pervert'. Poor bloke, he is stunned but that isn't the worst of it. She then launched a clenched fist in his direction. Whacked him right in the face. Poor sod. So for his troubles Bob leaves the ward stinking of shit, with a black eye, a buggered back. You can't make it up."

Rick started to chuckle to himself and then before long the both of them fall about laughing heartily at old Bob's misfortune.

"He won't be coming back to the ward in a hurry, poor bloke, and I won't be on his Christmas card list for sure. You know, I am sure the public have no idea what we have to go through."

"Umm, I think you're right, Sister Alicia. Bob deserves a medal. He'll probably get slated by the boys for getting beaten up by an old lady as well." Rick chortled at the thought of it. "Anyhow, Alicia, that's one down, what about the remaining 24 patients on the ward? Any other traumas in your day?"

"Well that one was quite funny really in a gross sort of way. The ward rounds were all finished without too much trauma, even our friend Henry H was not too critical today. He certainly seems to be mellowing in his old age. By the way, you know that Phyllis has a thing for him, don't you?" Alicia chuckled.

"Phyllis… as in our receptionist… likes a bit of lippy… pouts-a-bit Phyllis?"

"The very same and the pouting is mainly directed at Henry H."

"Blimey, how does he react?" Rick raised his eyebrows.

"Well to be honest I think he is starting to enjoy it."

"Well I'll be damned. Hoorah Henry and Phyllis. What a combination. Well they say love is a funny old thing, but you know, good for them, hope it works out. Anyhow, you were telling me… what was next in your awful day? So far on the scale of awfulness you have reached about six. What tipped it to ten out of ten for true awfulness?" Rick took a sip of his wine and looked attentively at his visitor.

"Well it was the usual story in so far as Mrs Taylor's admission. Her residential home clearly couldn't cope with her and so they sent her to us on the pretext that she had abdominal pain. So as well as having to deal with her unfortunate incontinence, she blocked my last acute surgical bed and we had to close the ward to any more surgical admissions." Alicia raised her eyebrows in an expressive frown. "Well then I got verbal abuse from the bed manager who said that she's got patients waiting in A&E to come up for admission to the ward."

"Blimey, is that Barbara, the bed manager?" Rick piped in.

"The very same – bark and bite equivalent... so I hear. Anyhow, I explained the situation to her and she still gave me grief. So Phyllis grabbed the phone and asked, 'Where the bloody hell do you want us to put these patients? Sit them on the toilet with an IV drip? Mattress on the floor?'"

"Oh dear, I bet that went down like a lead balloon. Mind you, an interesting battle, Phyllis versus Barbara the bed manager." Rick grinned.

"Well, it all got a bit heated and I had to calm everyone down. But Rick, you know the truth is we just do not have enough beds, let alone staff. These bed blockers don't help, patients are turned away or queuing up in A&E and then everyone gets stressed out… patients, relatives and especially our staff. I guess because it matters to them how patients are looked after. They just want caring competent nursing for them."

Rick nodded. He admired how much she seemed to care and how passionate she was about the NHS. It was Alicia's turn to have a sip of her wine and Rick couldn't take his eyes off her. She was quite the most adorable person he had ever met.

"Are you staring at me?" Alicia chuckled.

"Yes… um, sorry."

"I can only assume that is a good thing, unless I have dribbled red wine somewhere I shouldn't have."

"No, no. Alicia, it is because you are… lovely." There was no awkwardness when he spoke, just simply a heartfelt response and she knew he was sincere. She reached across and kissed him gently on the cheek.

"What was that for?"

"Just returning the compliment." They both laughed. There was a bleep from Rick's phone.

"You are not on call are you?" Alicia enquired. She looked disappointed.

"No way! Not tonight, not me. That, dear lady, is my phone's timer, the pizza is ready," Rick laughed, and sure enough the delicious aroma of one of Rick's favourite ready meals wafted through from the kitchen. "Ah… it's great, pizza. Do fancy a bit?" Rick raised an eyebrow.

"You are very forward, you know. A slice of pizza would be fabulous. Thank you." She laughed as she said it, as did he. They both talked on about their respective days, the trials and tribulations of work, the patients they looked after and the numerous characters they encountered. They both laughed a lot, shared and empathised with each other. Soon the pizza was gone and the bottle of red wine depleted and still they chatted on.

Alicia thought to herself as she watched him chatting away, how easy he was to talk to and how good he made her feel. He seemed genuinely interested in her and what she had to say. He even laughed at her jokes, but remained respectful of her and her views; he seemed to value her opinion which was great for her own self-esteem.

The clock in the hall chimed midnight. Rick glanced at his watch to confirm the time as he really didn't want this to end. He had really enjoyed her company and could so easily have gathered her up in his arms and asked her to stay. Mentally, they had just clicked and her care, generosity and human warmth endeared her to him. The person that she was enhanced her physical attractiveness even more and Rick wanted nothing more than the joy of physical intimacy with this gorgeous woman. Yet something held him back, it was too early and he didn't want to spoil anything.

For her part, Alicia felt so at home and comfortable with him. She trusted him implicitly and instinctively knew that he was a decent man. More than that, she fancied the pants off him. Their respective senses of humour just seemed to click; they had laughed out loud at the same things and she contemplated how rare it was to find someone that you just connected with. It was all so different to a recent experience of hers, a previous relationship that had gone so badly wrong. Her ex-partner who had outwardly been a respected solicitor, had proved to be a control freak who in the end had become abusive. It had taken all of her courage to end this toxic relationship. She was now so relieved to be out of it and had sworn to herself that she would never again be beholden to any such man… and here she was again, what the hell was she doing? Alicia snapped out of her current mindset.

"Crikey, look at the time. Rick, thank you so much for a lovely evening. I am on an early in the morning. I'd better go and get some beauty sleep." She suddenly became a bit matter-of-fact and it startled Rick.

"Oh, of course. I really enjoyed this evening too Alicia. Thank you so much for coming over and for the wine. We should do it again soon." He walked her to the hall and with one hand on the front door, he leant in to kiss her on the mouth, but she turned and presented her cheek.

"Goodnight Rick, and thank you." She turned her eyes away from his rather confused gaze.

"Oh. Goodnight Alicia."

CHAPTER 7

After a further week on the psychiatric unit, Mrs
Joyce Evans had been deemed fit with regard to her
psychological status and had subsequently been
discharged and allowed home with regular CPN
(Community Psychiatric Nurse) follow-up. She had
returned to her own house and had found it
devastatingly lonely after the busy psychiatric ward.
Joyce busied herself with cooking, cleaning and
running the inevitable errands for the WRVS. She had
immersed herself in whatever activities were on offer
to try and forget about her little dog and more than
that, the man who had been the cause of his demise.
Following the realisation that it had been Dick who
had thrown Geoffrey from the top of the hospital to
his death, Joyce had become withdrawn and cold to
the old airman, although fortunately the upset had not
delayed the return of her sanity, if anything it had

made things clearer in her own mind. At least now she knew that Geoffrey had not been cold-bloodedly murdered, his unfortunate death had resulted from the illness of a dear and kind man, but still she could not forgive Dick. For Dick's part, despite his earnest apologies and perfectly reasonable explanations that he was ill when such unfortunate events unfolded, yet still his pleas for pardon went unanswered.

Joyce was on a mission to scrub her little house until it was immaculate; not a particle of dust could be found on any piece of furniture, and not a cushion was out of place. A paint brush remedied any hint of scuffs and deficiencies with regard to the décor of the little Victorian terrace, and the windows gleamed. Joyce's garden was lavished with meticulous attention; no weed stood a chance of any sort of life and was ruthlessly and efficiently removed. The pond was re-stocked, the lawn fed and the shrubs lovingly nurtured.

When there was no more to be done, Joyce would sit in her little garden, alone and hurting. The absence of activity forced her to reflect on the meaning of her life and in particular how lonely she was. The death of her little dog had been traumatic, but not for its own sake, but because it was the final straw in the stark realisation of the perceived emptiness of her own life. A life that had on many occasions blocked out the affection of others and never allowed any human being to gain a foothold in her own ordered existence because of the fear of ultimate rejection and loss of propriety. Joyce had lived through a very strict childhood where emotions were stifled, sex was seen as a sin, and perceived respectability was all important. When she had been ill, she had allowed Dick a faint glimpse of the real person underneath her façade of respectability – for indeed she was as passionate and needy of love as the next person. She had found herself surprisingly excited and elated at his attention. She had at first been disbelieving that he found her attractive, but this had changed the more she got to know him. Then Joyce had found solace and felt safe in his frequent defence of her whilst an inpatient and allowed him to see a glimpse of the warm person beneath the façade. But she became ever more anxious the closer he became, and her fear of hurtful rejection took hold. The truth surrounding her little dog's death was her escape route from taking a chance in life and letting Dick in.

So she remained within a prison of her own making. She missed her work, but had decided early retirement was appropriate. In truth, she could not return to work in the hospital where she had been an inpatient, and the stigma of her psychiatric admission added to an imaginary shame. Dick continued to try and make contact with telephone calls and sweetly written cards, but these she ignored, until they finally stopped. And then one morning a sequence of events unfolded that would change her life forever.

Joyce got up as usual at 0730 hours precisely. She made her bed in meticulous fashion, then went to her bathroom to wash. To her surprise and horror, during the course of her ablutions, she noticed she was bleeding down below. It had been many years since she had menstruated and experienced 'period-like' blood loss and she knew straightaway the seriousness of her predicament. Postmenopausal bleeding was associated with cancer. She knew this all too well from her experience as a ward sister and now her mind played all sorts of tricks on her. Tears flowed, fear took hold and she felt ever more isolated.

That same morning she tried to make an appointment with her GP, but was unable to get through on the telephone. So she decided to walk in the pouring rain to the surgery and arrived completely drenched. On approaching the counter, an officious-looking receptionist failed to even acknowledge her. Joyce cleared her throat.

"Um, excuse me please, I wonder if I can have an

appointment to see one of the doctors?" There was no response. In a previous life as a ward sister, Joyce would not have tolerated such insolence and rudeness, but age and her recent traumas now got the better of her, sapping her self-confidence and making her timid. She again quietly repeated her request.

"What?!" The discourtesy from the receptionist was almost unbelievable.

For the third time Joyce politely requested, "Please, is it possible to see one of the doctors?"

"We are very busy, you know. What is wrong with you and why do you need to see the doctor?"

Joyce was stunned into silence. She was not about to share with this woman and indeed the entirety of the waiting room, who had now turned to look and listen to the exchange, the fact that she was suffering with bleeding of a rather intimate nature. She forced the tears back and didn't quite know what to do or say. She started to stutter.

The ill-mannered receptionist took full advantage, "Well it can't be that bad…" until she herself was cut off by a firm male voice coming from behind Joyce.

"Forgive me for interrupting, but do you know you are unbelievable? To ask any patient why they need to see the doctor is between the doctor and his patient – it is not common information to be blurted out for the whole of the waiting room to hear. This lady is a senior nurse at our local hospital and if she wants to see a doctor, there will be a bloody good reason for it. So please sort it out." It was Dick Chambers' unmistakeable and reassuring voice and Joyce's heart missed a beat.

It was now the turn of the receptionist to become unsure of herself. She turned scarlet, particularly when the whole of the waiting room nodded their agreement of Dick's protestations. At that point the local GP who had overheard the whole debacle from the open door of her consulting room, came out and over to the reception desk. She frowned disapprovingly at her discourteous member of staff.

"I'll speak to you later." The GP looked thunderously at the chastised receptionist before she turned to Joyce and smiling said, "Please excuse the ill-mannered way in which you were dealt with. Sister Evans, isn't it? You were marvellous to my mother when she was an inpatient on Bedlam ward. I am Dr Elizabeth Lewis, please do come with me." With that Joyce started to follow the kindly GP into her consulting room, but before doing so she turned, looked at Dick and with a relieved smile mimed, 'Thank you.'

Dick nodded. While the lovely GP had been remonstrating with her receptionist, he had scribbled something onto a scrap of paper and unashamedly walked up to Joyce and pressed it into her hand before he quietly whispered, "Good luck." Joyce followed Dr Elizabeth Lewis into her consulting room and closed the door.

Dr Lewis took a full history and then completed a thorough examination of her patient, before sitting Joyce down and explaining to her the possibilities behind her current symptoms.

"Joyce... if I may call you that instead of Miss Evans?"

"Yes, of course Dr Lewis," Joyce responded.

"Clinical examination is essentially normal and in particular, the neck of your womb or cervix looks normal which isn't surprising since all of your smears have been normal in the past. However, I cannot see into your womb which is the likely source of the bleeding and so I am going to refer you to my colleague Mr Rick Donovan, one of the consultant gynaecologists up at the hospital. Is that OK?"

Joyce nodded. "Thank you so much, Doctor, and thank you for seeing me so quickly. Your kindness is much appreciated."

"Joyce, it is an absolute pleasure. I'll do the referral this morning and we'll organise a scan. Hopefully you will be seen in the next seven to ten days up at the hospital. Remember ninety percent of the time this is nothing to worry about, but we need to check everything out."

The receptionist looked extremely sheepish when Joyce came out of the consulting room. Joyce marched up to the desk looked her in the eye. "One day perhaps you will be unwell and scared, I only hope that the people you come across in your future attempts to seek help are more caring and considerate than you have been to me." Joyce spoke with a sadness in her voice that was not judgemental but encouraged reflection. Duly chastised, the woman at the desk apologised unreservedly and as far as Joyce could tell, the apology was sincere. Joyce was gracious enough to accept it with the hope that a lesson had been learnt.

On her way out of the surgery, she looked around to see if she could see Dick. She wanted him to be there, to thank him once again for coming to her rescue. But he was nowhere to be seen. Then she remembered and felt around in her pocket for the scrap of paper that he had pressed into her hand. There it was. She took it out and read it.

I know that you may not want to be my friend,

And I cannot undo what I have done,

But I am here if you ever need me

Love,

Dick

He had scribbled his telephone number beneath the message. Joyce felt strangely elated and reassured. Why did this man keep popping up in her life? Perhaps she should call him just to say thank you again. When she arrived home she sat in front of her telephone with a cup of tea and willed herself to make that phone call. But every time she punched in the last number, she lost her courage and slammed the phone down. Perhaps tomorrow, she thought to herself.

Joyce received the appointment for a scan within a few days. She went into the scan room expecting to see a female sonographer and there sitting at the desk was a young man who looked like he had just graduated from high school. When he further explained that the sort of scan that she needed was a *transvaginal* or internal scan, she became a bit twitchy.

Sensing her unease, he carefully explained the

procedure for the scan and finished with, "It's all right, Miss Evans, I'll fetch a chaperone of course." The initial embarrassment of having such an intimate examination by a young man soon evaporated as his professionalism shone through. Ten days later Joyce found herself sitting with the scan result in front of Mr Rick Donovan.

"Hello Joyce. How lovely to see you again." Rick smiled warmly at her as she entered the consultation room and sat down. "Your GP has written to me telling me that you have had some bleeding, which of course is not quite normal after the menopause."

"Hello, Mr Donovan. It is good to see again too, although not quite so good under these circumstances." Joyce returned his greeting. She admired the young consultant and her experience of him as a clinician when she was ward sister of Bedlam, only served to increase her trust in him. After carefully explaining what he was going to do, Rick examined the retired ward sister with her consent and took a biopsy. He explained that the scan findings had shown that her lining of the womb was slightly thicker than it should be and of course that there was a possibility of cancerous cells being present. Joyce was already well informed and knew what the likely possibilities were. Rick informed her that the biopsy result would take about a week to be reported and that he would let her know the result as soon as it was back. He also explained that she would likely need another scan called an MRI; when she heard this she knew his thoughts on the matter. She said her polite goodbyes, declining the kindness of the clinic staff who offered her the inevitable cup of tea. She left the hospital and proceeded straight home. When her front door was closed behind her and she was alone, she burst into tears.

The next seven days that passed, predictably seemed like an eternity. Joyce spent them alone, distressed and fearful. Friends from her small social network including the WRVS rang and invited her to various functions, but she declined. Life for Miss Joyce Evans was reasonably grim and then it happened, unexpected and amazing.

The doorbell rang. She ignored it. Then it rang again and still she determined not to answer. When it rang for the third time, her resolve melted and she begrudgingly stomped to her front door and flung it open.

He stood there, a bunch of fresh daffodils in hand and an enormous smile on his face. Dick Chambers was not a man to be deterred.

"Hello Joyce, I thought you might need these." He pushed the flowers forward, carefully watching her face as he did so.

Joyce just stood there completely dumbfounded. A tear trickled down her cheek as she finally realised that the human being in front of her really did care. Her life sort of flashed in front of her. The strict upbringing, the hang-ups she experienced with regard to propriety, the disbelief that anyone could ever really love her, and now the possible diagnosis of cancer and with it the potential end of her very proper life. A safe life, lived without ever taking a chance, without ever letting anyone get close, a life lived without human love. At that moment with the diagnosis of cancer hanging over her, Miss Joyce Evans consciously decided to take a chance on life and finally live. She grabbed a somewhat startled Dick and hugged him close, weeping as she did so, exposing her true self to a man she was finally willing to take a chance on.

Dick in return was magnificent, he unequivocally accepted her into his arms and comforted her. No hesitation, just complete acceptance. Across the road, one of the neighbours stood gawping at her front door at the display of affection. There was a look of surprise with a hint of tut-tutting disapproval.

Through her tears, now of relief and exhilaration, Joyce spotted the busybody and surprising herself and indeed Dick, responded with an unqualified, "And you can piss off, you nosey cow, and mind your own business." The worm had turned.

CHAPTER 8

It was early morning. Rick had just got up. The image reflected in the mirror was not as pretty as it could have been. Rick sucked in his tummy, pushed out his chest and then relaxed again. Immediately his midriff flab discourteously hung once again over his pyjama bottoms.

"Umm, time for some exercise methinks," he said out loud to himself. "Perhaps take it easy on the beers, maybe even the curries and definitely no to the pizzas." He washed, shaved, put on his shirt and stumbled downstairs for breakfast, which today was a boiled egg, a few soldiers and a cup of tea. He was determined to avoid the enormous cooked breakfasts available from the hospital canteen and his ever-expanding gut confirmed this assertion. Since spring had finally arrived and the British weather had started to improve, Rick decided to get his bike out and cycle to work. He had heard some recent evidence on the radio that people who regularly cycle to work appeared to live longer, healthier lives (as long as they didn't get hit by a car). On the subject of healthier lives, he was due to be on call that night and the prospect did not fill him with joy. Rick let out a sigh of resignation in the knowledge that sleep deprivation had been shown to reduce life expectancy and increase levels of illness. Any health gain by his cycle ride would be shafted by his forthcoming night on call.

Rick Donovan had been part of that cohort of doctors who had, in days gone by, regularly worked up to 120 hours per week when jokes about medics falling asleep on patient beds were based on reality. He remembered one of his colleagues in the distant past who had been finishing a weekend shift; in the preceding 72 hours the unfortunate fellow had managed two hours' sleep and had still been at work. Towards the end of his shift, he had been asked to perform various blood tests on a number of patients, one of whom was extremely difficult to take blood from. It turned out that the poor gentleman concerned had been difficult to bleed, because he had in fact been dead, and the poor house officer had been so tired that he just hadn't noticed.

With these rather bizarre thoughts and recollections

going through his head, Rick donned his cycle helmet, strapped his briefcase to his bike rack and pushed his bicycle out of his front door. He glanced around at his next-door neighbours, but knew that Alicia should have already gone to work. Oddly, her curtains were still closed which he knew was unusual for her, since she was meticulously tidy and ordered. He hadn't seen her socially since the time they had shared a bottle of wine together and he had been left slightly confused by the encounter. The fact that she had pitched up at his front door, bottle of wine in hand and full of the joys of life, had been fantastic. The fact that he had not been able to kiss her properly or at least there had been a degree of reticence when he went to kiss her goodnight, suggested that all was not as he had hoped or thought.

It was a beautiful morning as Rick cycled into work. He thought he would take a shortcut through the park on the way to the hospital and was chuffed that he had done so. It was stunning. The trees were just starting to leaf, daffodils adorned and framed scattered bits of grassland as dog owners dutifully walked their array of mutts along the well-trodden paths. About 50 metres further on from where Rick was cycling, a couple sat on a park bench, not far from a small car park which lay beyond. They appeared to be arguing. She was slim, but had her back to him. He was young, well dressed, evidently some sort of professional fellow but he had an angry expression on his face and he appeared to be shouting at her. Although Rick was still a fair distance from where they sat, the woman looked familiar to him. He slowed down and continued to watch them. Weirdly it looked as she was trying to escape from her companion, but every time she made a move to leave he would pull her back, not in a well-mannered or gentle way but roughly. Rick's heart started to beat faster. He didn't like what he saw. As he got closer to the quarrelling couple, Rick squinted against the early morning sun, straining to see more clearly. She was wearing a hospital uniform under her coat. She again tried to get up from the bench and this time the man pulled her back down onto the seat and then to Rick's horror appeared to slap her across the face.

Rick could feel the anger rising within him. He cycled hard to the scene and the shock of the events unfolding in front of him was quadrupled when he realised who the woman was. When she turned slightly to avoid her aggressor's angry outpourings, she had tears rolling down both cheeks and a red mark on the side of her face where he had struck her. She looked up as Rick arrived at the bench, her eyes were full of fear and dread. It broke his heart to witness this, for in front of him, together with her assailant was none other than Alicia Granger.

"You're a brave man hitting a woman when she is clearly trying to get away from you. Hell, if I was her I would want to be as far away from you as possible, you schmuck." Rick was shaking as he flung his bicycle to the ground and confronted the man.

Alicia started to speak, "Rick please…"

Alicia's words were drowned out as her attacker stood up to face Rick. "Why don't you piss off, you arsehole, and mind your own business? Bugger off before you regret it." His face was contorted into a violent glare and his stance was that of an aggressor about to strike. His smart dress belied his thuggish manner, and now that Rick was close to him, he appeared menacingly large and his demeanour exuded a worrying confidence in the face of possible physical violence.

Rick gulped. Physical confrontation was not likely to result in an outcome which would be pleasing, especially to him. It would be a tad embarrassing if he got his arse kicked in front of Alicia. The gynaecologist changed tack. "You want me to piss off? I don't think so, old chap, you see the only one who is going to be pissing off, is you. I take it that you are aware that assault is likely to result in a prison sentence – probably not the best thing for your career and future prospects. Why don't we ask a friendly police officer what he thinks?" And with that Rick whipped out his mobile phone and pressed the emergency call button.

A well-aimed punch hit Rick on the side of the face and the shock of it made him drop his phone as he clutched his face in anguish. A second blow to the nose made him double over and drop to the ground. He was aware of the crunch of his mobile phone getting stamped on by his attacker. When he recovered himself enough to look up, all he could make out was Alicia being dragged towards the small car park where a solitary BMW was parked. She was crying, but there was now little resistance. The young consultant gynaecologist saw red. Fury welled up inside him and picking himself up, he ran determinedly towards the couple as they stepped into the car park. When he reached his assailant this time he had no fear, just blind rage.

Rick charged at the bigger man with a shout. "Just let her go, you bastard." Once again he was floored, but this time with a kick directed towards his genitals. If he thought the first few punches were excruciating, this was absolute agony. As Rick doubled over again, he could hear Alicia's screams and the sound of her scuffles as she tried in vain to put herself between this man and Rick as he crouched doubled up on the concrete path, now unable to move with pain.

"You think you're a real hero, don't you, you tosspot. Now I am going to make sure that your head is well and truly kicked in, pretty boy. What do you think of that… *old chap?*"

Rick was by now in too much pain to care about anything except his exquisitely sore gonads. But Alicia saw the murderous intent on the abuser's face and she prayed for miracle.

It came in the guise of a retired military officer by the name of Dick Chambers. He had been on his morning constitutional and to his disgust had clearly seen these unfortunate events unfolding. He had had the clarity of mind to start filming on his mobile phone and had already called the police. Dick walked with an old shooting stick, for the purpose of both a walking aid and because it enabled him to sit and ponder whenever he came across anything interesting on his strolls. As he ambled along, he gave the impression of a harmless old pensioner, such that although he had been spotted by all concerned, no one thought him a possible potential threat or indeed a potential saviour. How deceiving looks can be.

The thug's intent to kick a man already down was obvious, and as he was about to do so, a strong and purposeful voice resonated, "I wouldn't do that if I were you." Dick continued to film as he spoke.

"Ah God, another bloody hero, I suppose an old geezer like you is going sort me out too, eh? Sod it, old man, you can have a kicking just like your friend here," and the aggressor strode towards the old man with clear purpose. Rick could just about overhear and understand the overtones and as his attacker passed him towards Dick, he stuck out his foot. The action had the desired effect and the thug tripped and went flying, landing with a thud in the middle of a muddy puddle. As he went down, he smacked his nose on the ground and it bled profusely. His beautifully tailored suit was covered in mud and to add insult to injury, a dog turd adorned the lapel of his suit jacket and he now stank of dog shit. If it had been Rick's intention to cause maximum damage – he could not have done better. Rick, much to Alicia's horror, started to laugh out loud, his own bodily discomforts temporarily forgotten. The thug slowly started to get up with murderous intent on his face. He turned to where Rick was crouched, away from the old man.

"Not a good idea, shithead, now I *am* going to bloody kill you."

He moved slowly towards Rick, his fists clenched. Alicia ran forward and protectively placed herself in front of the gynaecologist. Then it happened. Dick proffered a well swung shooting stick to the back of the bully's head. The bully stumbled forward, dazed and collapsed into an even bigger pile of dog shit.

"I don't think you'll be killing anyone today, young fellow," Dick retorted and a police car with flashing blue lights swept around the corner into the car park and stopped in front of them. Two burly police officers got out. The scene that greeted them was not a pleasant one. A young woman in tears who had clearly been assaulted, one man crouched over clutching his nether regions, another just getting up, looking dazed and covered in dog poo and an older man with a shooting stick who looked like he was in control. The caller had certainly not reported a hoax.

The first police officer spoke. "Who is Dick Chambers?"

"That's me, Officer," Dick replied.

"OK, Mr Chambers, as you called us, please can you tell me what the hell has been going on here?"

"Certainly Officer, and thank you both for your very impressive response to a rather distasteful situation." Dick then with true military precision went on to briefly describe the current situation and the events leading up to the current time. He finished with, "And if there is any doubt about the validity of my story, I have it all recorded here on my phone."

On hearing Dick's account and the fact that there was video evidence, Alicia and Rick's assailant had started to get worried. Having recovered from his temporary dazed state, he had brushed himself off as best he could and then with a pleading voice tried to explain that he in fact was the victim.

"Officer please don't listen to that old man, I have just been seriously assaulted with a walking stick to the back of my head and make no mistake I will be pressing charges." As if to reinforce his statement, he gently brushed his fingers over the open cut on his scalp, wincing as he did so. With hand shaking, he dramatically turned his hand palm up to reveal fresh blood from his head wound.

"You liar! Officer, I swear to you this gentleman was only defending me from being attacked again, and I…"

Rick was cut short by the bigger of the two police

officers. "That's enough from everybody now, you can all come down to the station to make statements so we can get to the bottom of this, but in the meantime you in particular, what is your name?"

Everybody turned and looked around to the big, suited thug who had initiated the fracas. There was a look of panic on his face. "Why just me? They are the troublemakers, not me. Why don't you ask them their names?"

"I say again, sir, what is your name?" The policeman approached the bully and unclicked a pair handcuffs from his belt as he did so.

Alicia who had been silent up to that point spoke up. "His name his Jason Scott, I am ashamed to say that I used to be his girlfriend. He is a bully and an abuser and I want to report him for the physical and mental abuse that I have had to go through for the last six months. Please, Officer, believe me." Tears were rolling down her by now bruised face. She put her head into her hands and wept uncontrollably. It was evident to all concerned that Alicia was telling the truth and both the policemen looked upset at her suffering.

"You bloody bitch, fine bloody girlfriend you turned out to be." And Jason Scott without any warning ran towards her, fists flailing and hatred inscribed on his face. His turn of speed surprised them all, and his actions were so unpredictable that the policemen failed to move in time to prevent the attack. But the intended assault on Alicia never took place. Jason Scott's clenched knuckles never reached their target. It was Rick Donovan's flying rugby tackle that brought the big man down once again with a crash before he reached his intended target. This was all the police officers needed to know regarding the truth of the matter. Within seconds Mr Jason Scott had been handcuffed and put in the back of the Panda car. The man's swearing and abusive obscenities were ignored by all and only served to further convince the police what a nasty piece of work he was.

Alicia had wiped away her own tears and then ran to Rick's aid. He groaned in pain as she helped him up off the ground and guided him to the nearby bench to sit and get his breath.

"I'm so sorry, Rick, I never wanted you to get involved. Honestly, you should have cycled on, I would have been OK."

"Oh Alicia, with that abusive moron? I think not." Rick had started to regain his colour and his balls were aching slightly less, although his face ached. He moved his jaw up and down. "Ah well, nothing broken."

"Thank you, Rick Donovan. You are a wonderful man." And with that Alicia threw her arms around the gynaecologist and kissed him.

"Ouch, ouch, easy on the hugs please… although the kisses are quite soothing," Rick smirked. In truth he had quite enjoyed playing the hero, although he knew he would be sore for a while now. She kissed him again and they both laughed. Laughter of relief and on her part, laughter of gratitude.

Another voice joined in the chorus. "Well done, old chap, good tackle. I bet you were quite a rugby player in your day. What a bloody nasty bastard that chap was." Dick Chambers stood nearby leaning on his shooting stick. Rick and Alicia spun around to look at the unlikely protagonist who had literally saved the day.

"I know you." Rick looked closely at the man in front of him.

"And I know you, Mr Rick Donovan. You saved my life. Does the seventh floor of the hospital and another life-saving rugby tackle mean anything to you?"

"Oh my god… you. I thought you were admitted to the…"

"The psychiatric ward? Yes indeed, Mr Donovan… but now out and cured, and a different man. But I would certainly be dead if it were not for you. So my turn to say a very sincere thank you." Dick bowed graciously.

"Crikey, it's Dick… um… sorry I have forgotten your surname?"

"Chambers, Dick Chambers… at your service!"

"Well Mr. Chambers, I think the debt has been paid in full. Without your intervention that sadistic son of a bitch would have smashed my head in. So I, no, we," he looked at Alicia when he spoke, "owe you our thanks. We are indebted to you." It was Rick's turn to graciously nod his head.

"My god, this is like the mutual admiration society. Rather nice if you ask me. If I may be so bold as to express an obvious observation to you, miss." Dick looked down at Alicia. "I don't know how you got involved with such a misogynistic bully as the arse now sitting in the police car, but might I say that Mr Donovan here seems to me to be a much better sort of chap."

They all remained quiet as they got into a police van complete with Rick's bike and were transported to the local police station which was five minutes' drive from the park. Written statements concerning the events of that morning were required. As they travelled the short distance to the station, they all had a lot to think about.

CHAPTER 9

The police station was buzzing with activity. Colourful characters came and went with all shades, shapes and sizes of humanity being questioned, helped, arrested or cautioned by an equally colourful cast of police officers. Jason Scott was taken in handcuffs to an interrogation room and questioned extensively about the happenings of the morning. He told his story eloquently as would be expected of a practising solicitor, but not surprisingly his account of events differed significantly from that of Rick, Alicia and Dick. However, the video evidence from Dick's mobile phone was irrefutable and revealed Jason Scott to be a liar, albeit an accomplished one. When things had not gone his way, Mr. Scott simply flipped. For the first time in his life he was exposed for the criminal that he was. There was no hiding behind lies or fabrications, there was no exit through threats, bribes or cunning intimidation. It was at this point that Jason Scott basically lost control of his mind and his temper. To be arrested on the charge of multiple assaults was one thing, but thereafter breaking the nose of one of the questioning police officers in the interview room did nothing to endear Jason to his interrogators. In fact his psychopathic personality disorder had been exposed and then highlighted, particularly when Jason thereafter threatened to kill 'every last bastard' in the police station. The two officers in the same room with him, fearing for their lives, made a timely run for it and managed to get out in one piece before firmly bolting the reinforced door from the outside. They then called and waited for the unlucky psychiatric team to arrive. Following on from this, four plucky officers managed to physically restrain Mr Scott whilst the trembling psychiatrist administered a heavy sedative. The prisoner, gowned in a strait jacket, was transferred to a secure psychiatric establishment to await his fate, likely at a considerable cost to the average law-abiding and tax-paying citizen. But at least it was one less psychopath on the streets.

Mr Scott's aberrant behaviour, however, did have a number of positive aspects to it. Firstly the police were entirely convinced of both Rick and Dick's innocence. In fact they were full of praise for both of them coming to Alicia's aid and actually taking on such a violent nutter. Secondly, Alicia was informed that Mr Scott was likely to be banged up for a long period of time and therefore would be unable to bother her for the foreseeable future. And finally, Rick could now see the reason behind her previous cold feet when the two of them had seemed to click over a bottle of red wine. After being involved with and then trying to escape such an abusive personality, it wasn't really surprising that she would be reluctant to get deeply involved with anyone else.

The hours passed and finally the paperwork was completed. Alicia, Rick and Dick thanked the police officers involved and then made their way out of the station. Dick bade the young couple 'goodbye' and they in turn, once again expressed their sincere gratitude and thanks for his brave actions. He strode off, shooting stick at the ready, back to the park to complete his constitutional.

"Well Mr Donovan, just you and me."

"It looks that way, Miss Grainger, please allow me to escort you home."

"Oh Rick, what about work? I know that I am late but I really should…"

Rick looked at her, smiled and then countered, "Alicia, I have already rung the hospital manager and told them that you will not be in today."

Alicia looked directly into his eyes and let out a sigh of relief. "Thank you, in truth I am not sure that I could have coped with vomiting, diarrhoea and pustular wounds today, let alone Henry Horsham's ward round! Am sure I'll be fine tomorrow though. But Rick, thank you. Thank you for being so thoughtful and thank you for saving me from that man – if you can call him that. I am not sure how I can ever repay you. You may not know it, but you saved my life today." She breathed heavily as she spoke. It was a sigh of relief that the emotional and physical abuse was finally over.

They slowly walked back though the park, Rick wheeling his bike to one side. He had more or less recovered from the kick in the nuts, but a shiner had come up just under his left eye and his nose was a bit bloodied, all evidence of his gallant exploits. The sun was relatively high in the sky by now and it was a beautiful spring day. They walked silently, but contentedly, initially a little way apart, then closer together, then without a word she took his hand in her own. He gently accepted it as if it was the most natural thing in the world and wondered at the marvellous sensual intimacy of simply holding this woman's hand. The two of them strolled in the sunshine as if they belonged to each other.

They arrived back at Alicia's house. "Are you going to be OK now?" Rick turned and looked at her at the front door of her little terrace. His look of concern was endearing and she knew he was utterly sincere. She reached up and looking directly into his eyes kissed him sensuously on the mouth.

"I'll be absolutely fine and… thank you again." There was no hesitation, no doubt in her words or actions. He hugged her, gently kissed her on the cheek and then turned, clambered onto his push bike and gingerly cycled to work.

*

Bedlam ward was not quite as well organised and efficient without Sister Alicia Granger at the helm, but the senior staff nurse who was acting up was doing her best. She had just experienced a scolding from Mr. Henry Horsham as the observation charts on his postoperative patients were not completed satisfactorily. The unwitting nurse, however, was saved from Horsham's true wrath by Phyllis's intervention. The ward receptionist, armed with her most striking lippy surprised the entire team by interrupting the ward round to heap praise on Mr Horsham and inform him of the gratitude of a postoperative patient whose life he had recently saved.

The old surgeon had turned crimson with embarrassment, forgot that he was giving the senior staff nurse a bollocking, and proceeded with the rest of the ward round in an amicable and lamb-like fashion. Rick laughed on hearing these accounts when he later arrived to do his own ward round. He recalled what Alicia had said to him about Phyllis and Henry Horsham and it now seemed to make absolute sense. The receptionist really did seem to have a hold on him. Rick completed his rounds with minimum fuss and much to his relief, made his way to his afternoon gynaecology clinic.

The clinic started well enough. The first few patients were seen, assessed, examined and a plan of treatment for each was made that was agreeable to both patient and professional. Rick saw patients who had suffered with a range of diverse symptoms, everything from heavy debilitating bleeding, prolapsed genital organs, pelvic pain, infertility and of course cancer. Today was no exception to the assortment of conditions that Rick was faced with, and the next set of notes that were placed on his desk were those of Miss Joyce Evans. The notes had 'Staff' written across them and Rick recalled seeing Joyce the week before with postmenopausal bleeding. He had taken a biopsy at the time and organised an MRI scan. He now looked on the computer positioned on his desk to see if the result was available before he called her in. Sure enough the biopsy result was ready and Rick printed off the report before calling Joyce into the room.

"Hello Joyce, please come in and sit down." Rick offered the chair adjacent to his desk to the retired ward sister. "It is OK if I call you Joyce, isn't it? It's just easier and less formal than Miss Evans."

Joyce Evans smiled and nodded an affirmative. But she remained standing and then hesitated before softly asking, "I wonder if I might bring a friend in with me please?"

"Yes of course, please ask her to come in. It's always good to have a bit of moral support."

"Well actually, it is a *him* and you may already know him." And with that Joyce Evans stepped outside and called in her companion.

Not many things flabbergasted Rick Donovan, but he was to say the least, very surprised, no gobsmacked yet again that day. Dick Chambers strolled into the consulting room and sat down next to Joyce. He had changed from his walking clothes into a jacket and tie.

He smiled warmly at the dumbfounded gynaecologist.

"Um, good afternoon Mr Chambers. Good to see you again." Rick stuttered slightly as he spoke and wore a quizzical look on his face. It was not a look of disapproval, just one of pleasant disbelief.

"Good afternoon Mr Donovan, nice to see too. I hope you don't mind if I sit in with Joyce."

"Umm… no, not at all, in fact I was just saying to Joyce… it's always good to have some moral support." Rick then went on to introduce his clinical nurse specialist who would always sit in with him as a support for patients with cancer or suspected cancer. The gynaecologist settled down into his chair and picked up Joyce's notes. He looked straight at her and then spoke softly and empathetically.

"Joyce, the biopsy result is back and there is no easy way to tell you this, but it shows that there is an abnormality." Rick took a breath. It was never pleasant to give bad news, but experience had taught him just to get on and tell the truth. "That means that you have endometrial cancer." He paused and watched her face for some sort of response to the news that he had just given, or indeed to see whether she wished to interrupt with a question. Joyce's face remained stoically enquiring and concerned but her silence bade him continue with his explanation. He noticed, however, that she reached for Dick's hand and held it firmly. He found their affectionate liaison surprising but comforting. At least she wouldn't be alone for what was to come.

Rick continued, "There can be differing grades or aggressiveness of the cancer, and yours thankfully is a low grade or non-aggressive type. The special scan that you had, the MRI, also shows that it is likely that these abnormal cells do not appear to have spread anywhere else, but look as if they are confined to the inner part of the womb. So Joyce, there is no evidence from the scan that it has spread anywhere else."

A single tear betrayed her otherwise stiff upper lip. She held onto Dick's hand and then quietly asked, "Rick, we have worked for years together and you know me better than most. I am assuming that a hysterectomy is what is required, which is fine, but what are the chances of this thing coming back? Please just be completely straight with me."

Rick responded with a sincere smile, "Joyce, after working for years together you know me too. I tell it as it is. If you do not deal with the truth you cannot sort out the problem. The stats show that once you have been treated, you have a 98% chance of cure, pending confirmation of the biopsy following your surgery."

"So it's not a death sentence?" She probed, her anxiety lessening as the young gynaecologist further explained.

"No, far from it." Rick picked up the telephone and called his secretary. "Hi, when is the next available space in the diary for an urgent hysterectomy... Next week? Yes that sounds absolutely fine, thank you."

He put down the phone. "How are you set up for next week? We can fit you in next Thursday morning."

"Yes that's fine. Golly, that is really quick. I don't how to thank you enough."

Rick then proceeded to go over the details of the surgery. With pictures he showed the couple exactly what he was going to do. He then went over the potential risks associated with the surgery and what Joyce could expect following her hysterectomy. "Joyce, you know I cannot tell you 100% that this will result in a cure, but I can tell you that you are likely to be around for a long time yet." Rick smiled at the ex-ward sister. "Do you have any questions, or is there anything that we haven't spoken of?"

Then she did something completely out of character. Releasing Dick's hand, she got up from her chair and then threw her arms around the surprised gynaecologist. "Thank you Rick, I've gone from a death sentence to knowing that there is a great deal of hope. Thank you for explaining it all so clearly."

Joyce Evans and Dick Chambers left the consulting room like an old married couple. Dick nodded his thanks to Rick and all the staff as they left. They walked out of the hospital arm in arm. Her diagnosis had made her look at her life in a completely new way. It was as if the blinds to the reality of life with its previous constraints of false propriety had been lifted and she was no longer confined to her previous austere patterns of behaviour.

The couple walked along the streets of terraced houses until they finally reached Joyce's home. Opening the front gate, she led him up the short path to the front door.

"Cup of tea?" she enquired. "I have something I want to ask you."

"That would be lovely," Dick responded and followed her into the neat hall and on into the kitchen at the back of the house.

Joyce put the kettle on, made pot of tea and brought the tray through into the ornate and comfortable sitting room. She poured tea into two bone china cups and handed one to Dick. "Chocolate digestive?" she asked. He nodded.

The two of them were by now completely comfortable in each other's company. After all, they had experienced and seen each other at their very worst when they had initially become friends on the psychiatric ward. To get through and be supportive of one another at the lowest ebb in their lives meant that there was nothing to hide, just complete openness and with it a marvellous ability to just be oneself.

"Lovely cup of tea, thank you. Now Joyce, what is it that you wanted to ask me?" Dick ventured.

"Well, you and I have been through an awful lot together over these last few months and Dick Chambers, you have been wonderful to me. All my life I have been constricted in what I say or how I act for fear of immodesty or indecency. That is not to say that I disregard all propriety, there is a lot to be said for sober judgement and good manners, not to mention the importance of maintaining a good work ethic and moral standards. But my recent psychiatric illness and now this blasted cancer has shall we say, broadened my outlook. I find myself released from previous shackles that prevented me expressing my true feelings and indeed chasing happiness."

Dick listened attentively and intermittently nodded, encouraging Joyce to continue with her dialogue. Joyce then slightly hesitated; it would have been imperceptible to anyone else, but Dick had got to know her so well that he picked it up immediately. "Go on, please," he encouraged.

"Well, you see I know what I want. I never ever thought it would happen, and I never dreamed in a million years it would be me saying it, but Dick Chambers... I have fallen in love with you and..." she trembled ever so slightly as she took his hand again and looked directly into his astonished eyes, "and I wondered if you would do me the honour of being my husband?"

Dick didn't know what had hit him. He had certainly not expected that. The last year of his life flashed in front of him. The tumultuous time leading up to the death of his beloved wife Ann, his subsequent mourning and then mental illness, followed by his rehabilitation and meeting Joyce. She was most certainly a wonderful person and in truth he had fallen in love with her too, but... there was a slight pang of guilt at the prospect of getting married again. It was almost that if he were to accept Joyce's proposal, he would be somehow betraying his previous wonderful relationship to Ann.

Dick's hesitation in answering the question hit Joyce like a thunderbolt. She had not been quite sure where the question had come from. There had been no planning it. The bloody thing had just come completely out of the blue and had been entirely spontaneous. She withdrew her hands from his, the hurt in her face, palpable.

It took Dick a second or two before he grabbed both her hands back, and then looking into her eyes which was difficult by now since they were both openly weeping, spoke calmly and confidently. "My god… Joyce Evans you certainly know how to spring things on a chap! But darling, like you, I have fallen in love with the person in front of me and life is so short. Certainly you don't get many second chances in life and I am not letting you go… Yes, yes, yes, I would love to marry you."

CHAPTER 10

It seemed that the following week had flashed by in an instant and before she knew it Joyce Evans had returned to her old hospital, not as Sister-in-Charge, but as a patient awaiting her surgery. It was 7am when she arrived at the hospital as per her written instructions and Joyce had not slept a wink all night. It had been one thing spending years of her professional life looking after patients undergoing surgery, but quite another being on the 'other side' and actually being the recipient of surgical treatment. She knew all too well the possible complications of her forthcoming surgery but had every confidence in Mr Rick Donovan. Nevertheless, it didn't stop her having bouts of anxiety about the imminent knife to her skin.

Not surprisingly, Dick had been fantastically supportive of her and she really didn't know how she could have coped without him. The two of them had become closer and closer, and Joyce had been thrilled and elated at the newfound intimacy the two of them had shared. Her diagnosis had oddly also given her a confidence to express her own feelings and also the courage to accept the love of others. The week following her accepted proposal of marriage had been one full of laughter and love, despite her diagnosis. He had become ever more her trusted rock and support, and for the first time in her life she loved and was loved by a wonderful man.

Today was no exception to Dick's ongoing care and he insisted on accompanying her to Bedlam ward. He was not surprised to learn of the high esteem in which Joyce was held by members of staff within the hospital and although it was all too evident that she had been a taskmaster, albeit a fair one, there was also a great deal of respect and affection. As the couple approached the front reception desk of Bedlam ward, Phyllis greeted them with a broad welcoming smile and was soon joined by Sister Alicia Granger. They had reserved a side room for the ex-member of staff. Alicia had had the nod from Rick that Joyce and Dick were an item, and so Joyce was likely to be accompanied by him. As such, Alicia wasn't unduly surprised to see the couple walk arm in arm into Bedlam ward. She gave him a big welcoming smile to acknowledge his bravery and help from the previous week and then turning her attention to Joyce spoke with kindness and professionalism.

"Good morning both of you, we thought you might like a side room as opposed to the main ward. Joyce, it gives you a bit more privacy and it will be slightly easier when you have visitors." Alicia nodded at Dick.

"Thank you very much, Sister. That is very kind. Will Mr Donovan be coming around prior to surgery?" Joyce enquired.

"Absolutely, so too will the anaesthetist. Please let me introduce you to the staff nurse looking after you. This is staff nurse Jo Johnson, we all call her Jo. She will settle you in and take your observations." Alicia looked around and introduced the member of staff.

"Hello Jo, nice to meet you." Joyce smiled at the staff nurse.

"Thank you, good to meet you too. I'll let you sort out your things and then I'll be back to do your observations and fill in the paperwork if that is OK with you?" Jo beamed back.

Before Alicia and Jo turned to leave the side room, Alicia looked at Joyce. "If there is anything amiss or anything I can do, please just let me know. It's your turn to let us look after you now."

"Thank you," Joyce and Dick answered in unison.

Alicia left them to continue her other ward duties, prepare for the morning rounds and ensure all aspects of the running of Bedlam were in order. When everything was satisfactorily organised, she made her way to the ward office to sneak in a quick cup of coffee that Phyllis had kindly made her. There was the sound of muffled hilarity and laughter coming from within the office and as Alicia went in and joined Phyllis and some of her nursing colleagues, Jo Johnson was waving around a prosthetic breast to the hilarity of her colleagues who were laughing at her antics. Jo had recently returned to work following her diagnosis and subsequent treatment for breast cancer. She'd undergone surgery, followed by radiotherapy. She was one of the brightest and most optimistic people Alicia had ever met, hence assigning her to Joyce Evans.

Alicia thanked Phyllis for the coffee and then sitting down with the others asked, "OK Jo, what's the joke?" Alicia smirked as she asked.

"Well, Sister, I was just telling the girls about Bertha." She held up the prosthetic breast by the more than realistic nipple. "I was just explaining that every cloud has a silver lining!"

"How so?" Alicia looked quizzically at her staff nurse.

"I was telling the girls that last night my Bob was getting a bit frisky."

"Ummm, Jo do we need to know this?" Alicia was starting to feel sorry that she'd asked.

"Yes Sister, it's a laugh." Jo carried on with her story. "Anyhow, Bob carries on being all amorous and I really do not feel like it, being post-surgical and all. So when he says, 'Go on, girl, give us a quick feel,' I get old Bertha here out of the bedside drawer and give it him with, 'Here you are, Bob, have a fondle of that!'"

They all laughed heartily and Alicia marvelled at the bravery and wonderful self-deprecating humour of the middle-aged, yet young-hearted woman in front of them.

One of the other nurses spoke up. "Jo, if you don't mind I wonder if I could borrow Bertha? Sure beats a constant headache at bedtime. Perhaps we could buy a shed load, then rent them out for women with randy husbands?" They all laughed again, then finishing their coffees went back to the work of caring for their patients.

For Joyce, the rest of the morning consisted of signing consent forms, having her questions answered by an anaesthetist she thought young enough to be a schoolgirl, and then a review by Mr Rick Donovan prior to her hysterectomy.

Rick ensured that she fully understood all aspects of her forthcoming surgery before countersigning the consent form and answering any outstanding questions. Joyce's only complaint was the fact that she was both very hungry and thirsty, having had nothing to eat or drink since the night before. These pangs were not helped when Dick sat down in the side room and feasted on a piece of home-made carrot cake washed down with a nice cup of coffee, courtesy of Staff Nurse Jo Johnson. So when the theatre staff finally arrived to escort her to surgery, Joyce's tummy was rumbling both from lack of food and nerves. Dick tenderly kissed her goodbye, joking that he would see her when she got back with a refreshing cup of tea and her own piece of carrot cake. Then before she knew it she was accompanied off the ward, along the hospital corridor and on into the theatre complex.

The anaesthetic room was bristling with expensive technology, all very daunting even for an aged medical veteran like Joyce. Intravenous cannulas were skilfully inserted and an oxygen mask placed over her face. Joyce subdued a small panic attack when the young anaesthetist told her she was now just going to 'float off to sleep'. At that point, Rick put his head around the door, "All set? See you in an hour. Have a good sleep." She felt comforted by his confidence and then drifted off.

It seemed as if no time had passed at all before Joyce awoke into a hazy semi-conscious state. She was aware of a soothing male voice telling her that, "Your operation is all over and it went very well, take nice big breaths now, my lovely." Her abdomen ached slightly and she was somewhat nauseous, but other than that she felt OK and so very relieved that the surgery was all over. Sometime later she was transferred back to her own side room on the ward and there waiting for her was her beloved Dick Chambers. Sitting by the side of her bed, he took her hand in his own and spoke softly to her, reassuring words, kind words, loving words. Although in truth Joyce was drifting in and out of sleep for the first few hours and couldn't remember what he said – all she knew was that he was there for her.

Later that evening, Mr. Rick Donovan carried out a postoperative ward round and was accompanied by Sister Alicia Granger. The first patient that they reviewed was Joyce Evans. Dick had disappeared to get himself some supper from the hospital canteen. Joyce by now was very much awake and with it.

"Hello Joyce, how are you doing?" Rick looked down at his patient with a concerned face.

"I feel better than I was expecting to. Did it all go OK?" the ex-ward sister ventured.

"Absolutely fine and the good news is that there was no evidence of any cancer outside the womb. So hopefully everything is contained. Joyce, you know that we have to wait for the definitive histology to come back from the lab." Rick stopped when he noticed Joyce looking quizzically at him. "I'm sorry. By that I mean, wait until the pathologists have looked under the microscope at your womb. Then we will know for sure that everything is contained, and fingers crossed, that will then mean a cure of your endometrial cancer." Rick stopped to ensure understanding in his patient's eyes.

Sensing all this was a bit overwhelming, Alicia interrupted, "Mr. Donovan, is it OK if we sort out a cup of tea for Joyce and perhaps a small piece of that fabulous carrot cake? She has been tolerating clear fluids up until now and I suspect would kill for a cuppa."

Rick got the message and then chuckled at how a cup of tea appears to cure all in British society. "Yes, of course, thank you Sister." Then consultant and ward sister proceeded to ensure that their patient's observations were normal and that her pain relief was adequate. As they left the side room, Dick arrived back on cue.

"Is she doing OK, Doc?" he enquired.

"Absolutely fine," Rick responded.

The following few days passed uneventfully and Joyce rapidly recovered. It was not long before her catheter was out and she was peeing, as well as mobilising, eating and drinking normally, and had achieved the all-important opening of her bowels. Despite her nurse training, she had initially been somewhat reserved about telling anyone of her bowel habits, but when Rick Donovan joked that there was a prize for the patient who could fart the loudest and quickest, she soon relented. This was made easier when Dick, love him, purposefully let rip and apologised, for the sole purpose of ensuring she did not feel alone in the bowel habits department.

Joyce had been very impressed by the efficient manner in which Alicia ran her old ward, and admitted to Dick that she really could not have had better care. Alicia for her part ensured that her predecessor never had any cause to complain, partly out of professional pride, but also because the two of them had genuinely become quite fond of one another. When the ward had been quiet and Alicia had some time, she would sit with Joyce and they would share stories and experiences of the ups and downs, the highs and lows, the joy and sadness of being in the nursing profession. Dick visited the ward every day, bringing a single rose for Joyce and an array of biscuits, cakes and munchies for the nurses and doctors. He was always so bright and cheerful, bringing joy and laughter not only to Joyce, but to everyone he came across. When Alicia asked Joyce how they had met, the older woman told her of the whole saga, from when they met on the psychiatric ward to the present day. Joyce confided that having cancer had given her a new outlook on life and broken the chains of her previous suffocating conformity. She also confided that she had never been so happy as with this new and wonderful man.

Over the course of her hospital stay, many of her old ward colleagues came to visit and wish her well. Get Well cards adorned the little side room and were testament to the high regard and respect in which Sister Joyce Evans was held. The variety of visitors ranged from hospital porters, ward cleaners, nursing staff, and secretarial staff all the way to the senior surgical consultants. The fact that so many of her old colleagues seemed to care was wonderful; even Dick was impressed by the number of lives Joyce had obviously touched. One such visitor was Henry Horsham. Formally dressed in his suit and tie, he patiently knocked and waited at the side room door and only entered when there was an affirmative 'come in'. When he entered the little room he looked a little awkward, but did his best to give Joyce a warm smile.

"Thought I would pop in and say hello. I hear from Mr. Donovan that your surgery went according to plan. I was um, very pleased to hear that." The poor man looked ever so slightly awkward as he did his upmost to convey his best wishes to the ex-ward sister.

"Thank you so very much, Mr. Horsham. Very kind of you to come and see me," Joyce replied just as Dick came striding into the room. He was casually dressed in a pair of chinos and an open-neck shirt. Henry looked up, saw this stranger and armed only with the knowledge that Joyce had been a lifelong spinster decided that he was some sort of imposter.

"Excuse me, but who are you?"

"Hello, how do you do? I'm Dick Chambers, Joyce's worse half." Dick smiled as he spoke and offered his hand.

Henry was surprised and slightly taken aback. "Oh,

I see… um…. how do you do? I'm Henry Horsham, one of the surgical consultants." And with that Henry Horsham shook Dick's hand, but for some strange reason, reluctantly. He was even more astounded when Dick went up to Joyce and kissed her. He had known Sister Joyce Evans for 20 years and had to admit that seeing her here with this chap was almost alien to him, and so completely unexpected. In truth, it was something of a shock for the ageing consultant. Henry Horsham had been married to his work. He had ate, drunk and slept surgery to the exclusion of all else and had pre-supposed that his nursing colleague, whom he had known for the entirety of his professional working life, had done the same. But here she was, with this man, and as far as Henry could tell, Joyce despite just having undergone major surgery for cancer, was clearly a very happy woman. The whole scene underpinned and reminded Henry of the fact that there was no one special in his life. Just him and his work. It was extraordinary, but seeing Joyce here with Dick, suddenly and like a thunderbolt jolted his perception to the fact that he was so very much alone.

Joyce saw the confusion and somehow recognised the emotion in her old colleague. It was almost as if he needed more comforting than her. Over the years she had grown fond of the old surgeon, despite him being a real taskmaster at times. Now she empathised hugely with him, because in truth he was a very decent human being. He needed to take a chance in life, just as she had done. But what could she say to comfort him or prompt him into taking the bull by the horns and get on with real living? She knew that he would have to make that leap for himself and in the end, after a few more formal exchanges, Henry Horsham made his exit.

"Joyce, I just wanted to say… get well soon… and um, very pleased that all went well… and um, good to meet you Dick." He was clearly sincere, but looked slightly sad as he spoke.

"Thank you so much for coming to see me, Mr Horsham. It was very kind." Joyce smiled back. And then he was gone.

"Golly, he was quite formidable," Dick spoke, "reminded me of my old Wing Commander. Seemed a very formal, play by the rules sort of chap. I may be wrong but he looks like he needs to lighten up a bit, probably needs the love of a good woman. Did you see the look on his face when I kissed you? Thunderous, I thought he was going punch me!"

"Dick darling, don't be too hard on him. How

lucky was I to find you?" She took Dick's hand and gave it a squeeze. "He just needs to find the right one and then take a chance."

Little did she know what was coming.

*

It was Joyce's last night on the ward. After Rick Donovan's latest review, he had agreed to let her go home the following morning on the premise that Dick would stay with her, to look after her at least for the first week. Visiting time was over and the ward was quiet. Sometime later in the evening Joyce ventured out of her side room for a little walk. She wanted to ensure that she was able to mobilise a reasonable distance before returning home the following day. On her way out of the Bedlam, she passed the ward office, which was strangely closed. Stranger still, there were some rather disturbing noises coming from within. Groans and slurping sounds emanated from behind the closed door. Confused and then intrigued by such sounds, Joyce looked for a duty staff nurse but there were none to be seen. So she proceeded to turn the handle of the office door, fearing that perhaps someone was having an epileptic fit and needed help. Oddly the door was locked and the groans and slurping noises continued unabated.

"Oh my god, someone is dying in there," she whispered to herself. Then she remembered where they kept the spare key to the ward office. Holding onto her stitches she quickly retrieved the key from the front reception desk, and returning as fast as her postoperative state would allow, she put the key into the office door and turned the lock. Miraculously the moaning and sucking noises abruptly ceased, as Joyce pushed the door open and looked inside.

"Oh my god... Mr. Horsham...!" Joyce stood clutching the door handle for support, mouth agape, shock written all over her face. "And you... Phyllis... in the ward office?"

Henry Horsham was naked above the waist, Phyllis Jones was down to her underwear and appeared to be tugging at the very expensive leather belt around Mr Horsham's waist. Joyce assumed that the sucking noises had been a result of some sort of primordial kissing ritual.

Following their rather unexpected exposure, the only word that Phyllis could come up with was, "Oops."

Henry Horsham on the other hand had turned white as a sheet; he rapidly untangled himself from the ward receptionist and grabbed his shirt to cover his naked torso. He could see the possible consequences of his current behaviour leading to years of dedicated hard work going up in smoke, and his career coming to an abrupt and disgraceful end. To be caught having nookie in the ward office with the receptionist would not only lead to his professional demise but would likely make him a laughing stock. Yet admirably, his first concern was not for himself, but for Phyllis and her good name, although Joyce could have told him that Phyllis was a very much a wolf in sheep's clothing. But then again, perhaps Phyllis was just what he needed.

The old surgeon looked sheepishly at Joyce who by now had firmly closed the door behind her to ensure no other party was privy to the sordid scene.

"Joyce, I am so sorry that you found us like this. I know how completely unprofessional this is. But this is my doing, not Phyllis, I want to make that clear… I…" Horsham was almost crying when he spoke, and Joyce knew exactly what was going through his mind. She was not about to let the career of a wonderful surgeon go down the pan because of one silly misjudgement.

"Henry Horsham, just stop talking for one minute." Both Henry and Phyllis were by now fully dressed and sitting to attention as the ex-Sister Joyce Evans presided. "You are clearly equally to blame for this ridiculous and Neanderthal behaviour and I strongly suspect that it was you Phyllis, who instigated this unsavoury debacle", then looking wistful Joyce continued, "You both are as guilty as my darling Geoffrey used to be when he had stolen a sausage from the side board."

Neither Phyllis or Henry were entirely sure of the relevance of the deceased dog and sausage analogy, but nevertheless Joyce was both judge and jury, and executioner if she so wished, so they kept quiet and waited for her to continue. "This behaviour is clearly unacceptable and in days gone by I would have no choice but to report you both to the relevant authorities. Do you understand?"

Both Phyllis and Henry nodded.

"However, this is not my ward any longer and you are not my responsibility. In addition, I am not in the business of ruining respectable careers and reputations. So you will be relieved to know that this unfortunate incident will go no further than these four walls." Joyce took a deep breath in and before the accused in front of her could express their thanks, she continued, "Henry, I have known you for more than 20 years. Phyllis, I have known you a great deal shorter, however, I have been informed that you are diligent, hardworking, loyal and trustworthy. Now, when I see such obvious unbridled passion expressed in such a manner as I have just witnessed, I ask 'why?' so Henry, I ask you first, is Phyllis just a brief fling or have you fallen in love with her?"

Henry Horsham didn't quite know what to say, so he stuck with the truth, and looking directly at Phyllis answered, "Yes… from the very first time I met her – she refused to be intimidated and in fact gave me hell on ward rounds."

"Yes thank you… I don't want to hear the whole sordid story, and you Phyllis?"

Phyllis Jones returned his adoring look and simply said, "Yes, I love him."

"Thank God for that. Now I suggest that the two of you go and… get a room… and please, this behaviour is never to be repeated on hospital premises again. Do I make myself clear?"

The couple answered in unison, "Yes Sister," before exiting the office and disappearing from the ward. As he walked past her, Henry Horsham whispered, "Thank you Joyce, you have just saved my career and more importantly enriched my life."

CHAPTER 11

Some three weeks later, Joyce and Dick were sitting in the hospital outpatient waiting room waiting to see Mr Rick Donovan. The appointment was for the purpose of a postoperative review and the all-important results of the histology from Joyce's recent hysterectomy. The waiting room was full to capacity, the patients varied from the very old to the very young. The women waiting were of all shapes and sizes, with varying backgrounds from local cleaners to Managing Directors of big companies. The NHS catered and cared for the needs of everyone and there they all sat, patiently and some nervously, waiting in turn to be seen. Dick was chatting animatedly to a rather large, nervous lady sitting next him, when an automated call system requested Joyce Evans to go to Room 15. Joyce and Dick got up from their seats and proceeded to the appropriate consultation room. As they entered, Rick got up from his seat and with a broad smile, greeted them both with a firm handshake.

"Lovely to see you both again. Joyce, if you don't mind me saying so… you look fantastic. Please sit down, both of you."

Joyce had indeed made something of a miraculous recovery from her surgery. She walked confidently into the room, looking happy and healthy. Rick marvelled at the difference between her and some of his other patients. The gynaecologist knew that her positive outlook, together with support both emotional and physical that Dick had showered upon her was responsible for her wellbeing. Nevertheless, he also detected the worry in her eyes about the forthcoming biopsy result from her surgery. He knew that she would be fretting that the cancer was advanced or indeed had spread, or that she would possibly need further treatment such as chemo or radiotherapy. Rick quickly got straight to the point. He turned the computer screen on his desk towards the seated couple and spoke while confirming his words with the written report on the computer screen.

"Joyce, it is good news. The cancer was confined to the lining of your womb and *nowhere* else. Also, it is what we call a low grade cancer which means that it is not an aggressive type. The statistics indicate that now you have had your surgery, you have a 98 percent cure rate." Rick had barely finished his sentence, before his the ex-ward sister had got up and flung her arms around him for the second time in less than two weeks. Tears of joy streamed from her eyes and when Rick looked up he saw that Dick too was tearful.

"Oh Mr Donovan, Rick… I, we don't know how to thank you. Thank you so much for your care… you have no idea."

But Rick Donovan had a very strong idea about the relief patients feel when told that their cancer has been successfully treated. He was also acutely aware of the difference a little human kindness makes. Treatment without compassion may have sorted out the physical side of disease, but human beings are more than just lumps of meat and a holistic approach to care was high on Rick's agenda. The gynaecologist reciprocated the couple's affections, then went on to ask about other aspects of his patient's postoperative recovery, which turned out to be most satisfactory.

Further follow-up was arranged for three months' time. When Rick then went on to say that he would be happy thereafter to discharge her because she was so "Low Risk", the couple were even more delighted.

As Joyce and Dick got up to leave, she turned once more to her gynaecologist.

"Oh, I have some news for you. Well, *we* have some news for you." Joyce then turned and looked unashamedly tenderly at Dick. She took his hand. "We are going to be married. I never thought it would ever happen, but it is, and it is the most marvellous thing in the world. We would very much like you to come to our wedding celebration?"

Rick wasn't surprised in the least that the two of them were going to tie the knot and was flattered to be asked to go to the wedding. "I'd be delighted to come, and thank you both for the kind invitation. Golly, this is turning out to be quite a day – love, marriage, clear of cancer. It is all no less than you deserve, Sister Joyce Evans… soon to be Mrs Joyce Chambers. That does have a nice ring to it!"

They all laughed, shook hands once again, before Joyce reached up and kissed Rick on the cheek. "The invite will be in the post and thank you again most sincerely."

Rick watched the two of them strolling down the corridor, hand in hand. He was so very happy for both of them. They had both had a rough time recently and deserved a bit of luck. Their freshly announced engagement led Rick to think about his own situation and feelings towards Alicia. After the clinic was finished, Rick ambled back to Bedlam ward and was startled to see an array of medical and nursing staff running past him and on into the ward. Rick recognised them as the emergency crash team.

"Umm, some poor bugger has arrested, I had better take a look," he muttered under his breath.

On arriving on Bedlam, there was a clear frenzy of activity in the farthest bay from the entrance. Curtains had been partly closed around the bed and Rick could just about make out the 'Crash' team applying pads to the chest of the unfortunate individual. The unmistakeable sound of the defibrillator charging preceded the lead medic shouting, "Clear!" before the 360 joules of energy were pumped into the unfortunate individual. In the meantime, intravenous lines and various drugs had been administered and oxygen applied. Rick saw the body jump on the bed when the shock was applied, and then the continuation of life-saving resuscitation. The cycle was repeated before finally the lead medic called a halt. The team's eyes focused on the heart rhythm screen in front of them. The relief on their faces was testament to a successful resuscitation and the human being behind that curtain had been saved from an eternal sleep on that day at least. It turned out that the fortunate or unfortunate person on the receiving end of CPR was a Mr Harry Johnston. He was 79 years of age. From behind the curtain surrounding his bed, walked Sister Alicia Granger; she was clearly flushed from the effort of doing chest compressions, but mightily relieved of the successful outcome. She saw Rick and smiled.

"Not one of yours, Mr Donovan, you'll be pleased to know."

"I should hope not, Sister, not in the male bay anyway! But well done you. That all sounded very professional and the end result is testament to its effectiveness." Rick walked with her to the ward office.

The telephone rang. Rick watched as Alicia picked up the phone and answered, "Bedlam ward, Sister Granger speaking, can I help you?" The telephone was on speaker mode.

"Hello dear. This is Mrs Mary Johnston speaking. I am phoning to ask how my Harry is getting on, Harry Johnston." The voice sounded like that of a dear old woman.

"Oh, right, Mrs Johnston. Well I am afraid your husband has taken a turn for the worse." Alicia tried her very best to be empathetic.

"My husband! He is not my husband, he is my son!" The old lady was clearly displeased.

"Oh, I do beg your pardon, it was just that since Mr Johnston is nearly 80, I had assumed that…" Alicia was now choosing her words very carefully. Rick had started to chuckle at his colleague's discomfort. Alicia continued, "Forgive me, it is just that you sound so young on the telephone I immediately assumed you could possibly be Mr Johnston's wife, but clearly it is an assumption that I should not have made, and I do apologise."

The cocktail of flattery and apology did the job and before long, Mr Johnston's mother was eating out of the ward sister's hand. It turned out that the old lady herself was 98 years young and there was nothing wrong with *her* brain. She listened intently to Alicia's explanation and subsequent reassurance about her son and at the end of the conversation thanked Alicia 'from the bottom of my heart', and with a 'bless you, dear' before the receiver was finally put down. Rick had listened to the whole telephone exchange and realised just how fantastic the woman standing in front of him was. He had watched how her wonderful emotional intelligence, diplomacy and evidently caring nature turned a tricky situation into a calm and comforting dialogue. It was a masterclass in positive human interaction and Rick at that moment just knew.

"Crikey, never thought an 80-year-old man's mum would phone to see how her 'young' son is getting on! Serves me right for being ageist!" When Alicia chuckled, her eyes lit up and the goodness of her heart shone through.

"Quite. Now, Sister Alicia. I have had a really good day thus far, and was wondering if you would make it even better by agreeing to have dinner with me tonight?"

"That would be lovely, thank you Rick. I finish my shift about seven tonight. What's the occasion?"

"Well that would be telling. I suppose… firstly, just an effort to improve neighbourly relations by treating my next-door neighbour to a fabulous, well-deserved, slap-up meal and a glass of wine or two. It helps the community spirit, don't you know," Rick mocked.

"Do you take all your neighbours out for dinner to foster good community relations?" Alicia supressed a poorly disguised giggle.

"Only the good-looking female ones, with the body shape of a goddess!" Rick countered. "Of course it will mean the aforementioned deity having

170

to suffer my company, if you are up for it?" Rick hesitated, then continued, "And anyhow, there is something that I want to ask you."

"Blimey, that sounds a bit risky!" she chuckled.

He blushed. "I'll book the table. Do you like Moroccan and Lebanese food?"

"Sounds great!"

"OK, next question. Do you know '*The Kafta and Kibbeh*'? It's a fantastic Moroccan restaurant not far from us," Rick asked.

"Oh, I know," Alicia replied, "I've noticed it on my way to work. It looks fabulous and always busy. Don't they have a belly dancer performing?"

"Absolutely." Rick raised his eyebrows. "Should be fun, so put your best glad rags on and I'll pick you up about eight-ish?"

"Fantastic, I look forward to it," she smiled and then got back to the job of caring for her patients.

CHAPTER 12

At eight o'clock sharp, Rick found himself standing at his next-door neighbour's front door. He rang the bell once and patiently waited. A few seconds later, Alicia stood in the doorway looking stunning. Rick leant forward and kissed her on the cheek and as he did so picked up the faint, alluring, subtle aroma of *Chanel 19*.

"You look beautiful," he said.

She smiled. "You're not so bad yourself, Mr Donovan. I think neighbourly relations are definitely on the up."

They both laughed. He took her arm and they strolled the two blocks to the '*The Kafta and Kibbeh*'.

They were shown to a candlelit table for two by a rather effeminate, bearded waiter called Waleed. In a gentle voice, Waleed bid them both a 'good evening' and then proceeded with, "I can see for you this is a most amorous evening, and Waleed is going to make it very special. As your waiter tonight, your wish is my command."

Rick raised his eyebrows but thanked the acquiescent waiter for his attention. He ordered two beers and a bowl of olives and then he and Alicia studied the menu. Waleed brought the drinks over in record time and then delivered a bowl of succulent olives. Then in a heavily accented voice, Waleed interrupted the diners' conversation, leant over the table and in a conspiratorial tone whispered, "Where I come from, olives are the food of l-o-v-e, appropriate for you... do you not think?"

The waiter's question hung in the air, but Rick by now was getting a bit fed up. "Well Waleed, I am not sure about that, but olives certainly contain good quantities of Vitamin E, may be good for your heart and the oil is tremendous for treating constipation." There was a pause for effect, before Rick continued, "Now if you don't mind I'll begin with the *Harissa Humus* as a starter, then move onto the *Lamb Bourak* for my main course. Please may I also have a bottle of your best house red?" Then looking across at Alicia with a wink and a chuckle, he asked, "Darling, my voluptuous angel, vision of loveliness and light of my life… are you ready to order?"

Alicia played along, and looking adoringly into Rick's eyes, "Of course, my cherub. I too will have the *Harissa Humus* to start, and then for my main course, the *Sajuk and Halloumi*." She turned to the bemused waiter, fluttering her eyelids. "And not that we need them but just in case perhaps another bowl of your *love* olives, you wonderful Waleed?"

By now Waleed was not quite so sure of himself and having efficiently delivered their food and wine, then a further bottle of red wine, he made himself scarce, much to the amusement of Rick and Alicia. After a couple more glasses of the red stuff, the conversation really started to flow between the two of them. They spoke of their respective work, patients that they had known and looked after, and the difficulties of developing anything within the bureaucratic confines of the NHS. They both shared stories of joy at successfully treating difficult cases and the privilege of sharing and having an insight into their patients' lives. Equally, they spoke empathetically about the patients who had not done so well and the trauma this entailed for all concerned. They reminisced about family, friends and good times with a rollercoaster of emotions from joy and laughter to sadness and regret. Throughout this, Rick watched her as she spoke, the fine rich lines of her mouth, the vivacity in her eyes, the way she swept back her tousled hair after leaning forward to laugh and the manner in which she would listen to him, looking directly into his eyes without timidity or embarrassment, her chin resting on a delicately flexed hand. For her part, Alicia had never felt so safe and it enabled her to be completely herself, without fear of being judged or misunderstood. She in return watched the man sitting opposite her. He was not conventionally what you would call handsome, although he was still physically striking. It was the kindness in his eyes, his sense of fun and the charismatic nature of his personality that made him hugely attractive. Whilst she was studying his face as they talked and laughed, their eyes met and for an instant neither of them said anything, but were just transfixed in the moment. There was a knowing, almost a recognition between them of a found kindred spirit.

The moment was broken, when the restaurant loud speaker system kicked in to announce that their most exotic, erotic and flexible belly dancer, Asya, was going to perform her locally famous *Oryantal* and moments later an energetic young woman dressed in a *Bedlah* burst out onto the restaurant floor and started her belly dance routine to the music, *Basbousa*. Asya was an instant hit especially with the male diners as she cavorted around the tables with almost unbelievable agility and nimbleness. She arrived at one table adjacent to Rick and Alicia's and her gyrating belly button complete with piercings had managed to totally transfix the gentleman at that table, who was now having great difficulty finishing his soup. The woman accompanying him, who Rick and Alicia took to be his wife, was clearly not at all pleased and looked daggers across the table at him. The gentleman concerned was suitably chastised and subsequently tried but failed to divert his lustful gaze away from Asya's voluptuous curves and thrusting hips. An inconspicuous kick in the shins under the table from his red-faced beloved wife seem to do the trick and also proved to be the hint for Asya to move on to the next table. She gracefully danced in front of Rick and Alicia, and together they laughed and clapped to her wonderful suppleness. Asya recognised her chance to persuade a diner to dance with her and offered her hand to Rick to join her.

Rick felt slightly uncomfortable, looked sheepishly at Alicia to ensure she was OK with this and when he saw her laughing and encouraging him to get up, he threw caution to the wind, stood up and belly danced to his best ability around the restaurant with the beautiful young woman. Rick's fellow diners all started to clap and holler at the gynaecologist's best efforts and before long it was Rick who was the centre of attention with his gyrating hips and ingratiating smile. He gyrated back to his table where he grabbed Alicia's hand and pulled her up from her chair. She was magnificent, throwing herself into the fun of the occasion and belly danced almost as well as Asya. When the music finally came to an end, the whole restaurant was clapping and cheering and Rick taking Alicia into his arms, held her then kissed her. Another cheer went up and the couple turned and bowed, before sitting down at their own table, laughing and totally out of breath.

"Wow, Mr Donovan, you have certainly got some movement in those hips of yours!" Alicia exclaimed. "Does your gift have any useful applications in any other aspect of your life?"

"Alicia Granger, really! That's for me to know and you to find out!" Rick laughed.

A short time later, Asya reappeared at their table with two complimentary glasses of *Raki*. "Courtesy of the house for being such good sports and wow! Talk about rubber hips and wonder thrust. If you guys ever need a job here… let me know." The young dancer chuckled to herself and then addressing Alicia, whispered in a conspiratorial tone, "If I were you, I'd keep this one, love," and with that she pursed her full lips, blew Rick a kiss and was gone.

"You've got a fan there, Mr Donovan," Alicia giggled.

"Um, think I'll stick to present company if that's OK with you?"

"I was rather hoping you'd say that," and Alicia lifted her glass of complimentary *Raki*. "Cheers, here's to us!" And they both downed the *Raki*.

The couple shared a tasty dessert of *Baklava*, before Rick gestured to Waleed and ordered coffee. The waiter duly complied and on placing the coffees on their table each with a piece of Turkish delight, turned to Rick with an enormous grin and softly spoke, "Impressive dancing, sir; you and madam are very gifted."

"Thank you Waleed, very kind of you to say so and thank you for the coffee." As the waiter moved away, he joined the female chef who had just exited out of the door to the kitchen carrying a small birthday cake, complete with three lighted candles and two pieces of Turkish delight cut into the shape of love hearts. The two members of staff were joined by another waiter, who started to sing 'Happy Birthday' as the threesome advanced to the furthest and most inconspicuous table in the restaurant. The unsuspecting couple seated at the table looked up in horror to see the little procession closing in. They had chosen the most dimly lit and inconspicuous table in the restaurant in a futile attempt at discretion. The fact that the three very vocal members of staff from the *Kafta and Kibbeh* had encouraged the entire restaurant to sing along as they delivered the birthday cake did nothing to help matters.

Rick, who had previously paid little attention to the other diners, now gulped as he recognised none other than Mr Henry Horsham and Miss Phyllis Jones sitting sheepishly at the table in question.

"Well, well, well. I wouldn't have believed it. Looks like Phyllis nabbed her man, and old Henry looks like the cat who has got the cream," Rick whispered to Alicia under his breath. He watched as the birthday cake was placed on the table in front of his consultant colleague and the ward receptionist. The agony of the warbled 'Happy Birthday' singing finally came to an end before a round of applause went around the room. After a good deal of prompting from Phyllis, Henry Horsham finally relented and reluctantly blew out the candles on the cake in front of him. Henry was by nature, a very private man and outside the secure environment of his work, generally shunned attention especially in public, and all this open scrutiny was making him more and more uncomfortable. Phyllis leant across the table to kiss her man and another round of applause went up, but by now Henry was looking extremely pissed off. So when Phyllis picked up the heart-shaped Turkish delight and attempted to feed her beloved, his disinclination to accept her love offering was further heightened. But persistence held true as Phyllis almost stuffed the Turkish delight into Henry's mouth. The diners of The Kafta and Kibbeh all became riveted with the goings on at the lovebirds' table, and titters of laughter started to reverberate around the restaurant. Henry, who by now was red faced and extremely uncomfortable, chewed as fast as he could in the hope that his current predicament would quickly pass. But it was destined not to be.

Rick and Alicia watched in fascination as Phyllis reached across the table to ply Henry with the Turkish delight, but in doing so her blouse brushed over the lighted candle in the middle of the table. Phyllis started to smoulder and then promptly caught fire. She screamed as the flames caught hold and

Henry in a state of shock, inhaled the heart-shaped Turkish delight. Both reacted like a cat on a hot tin roof; in unison they sprung up from the table, pushing it over and its contents onto the restaurant floor. The quiet titters of laughter from fellow diners had turned into raucous laughter as Phyllis jumped around the room with a gasping Henry slapping her torso in a vain attempt to put out the blouse fire. The consultant surgeon was by now turning a disturbing shade of blue, and Rick knew it was time to take action. He grabbed a jug of water from his own table and with Alicia in hot pursuit ran over to the unfortunate couple. Rick threw the contents of the jug over his ward receptionist, while Alicia grabbed a breathless Henry Horsham and placing her arms around his midriff, carried out a more than competent Heimlich manoeuvre. The heart-shaped piece of Turkish delight flew with some force out of Henry's windpipe and into the eye of an unsuspecting Waleed. Waleed dropped his tray and its contents onto the floor of the restaurant and the crescendo of laughter around the room reached fever pitch.

Their humiliation complete, Henry who was still panting, and Phyllis soaked to the skin but otherwise unhurt, collapsed into each other's arms. Rick and Alicia stood to one side of them and a strange hush descended. Waleed had recovered his composure and now just stood dumbfounded, staring like everyone else in the place, at Henry and Phyllis. The couple in question then did something completely unexpected and marvellous. They turned, hand in hand to face the other diners, and took a bow. The place erupted with cheers, whistles and then a spontaneous round of applause.

It was not long before Phyllis was wearing one of the waitresses' logoed tops to replace her own singed blouse and preserve her modesty. Henry had recovered his breath and the four of them were sitting around a freshly laid table. Waleed brought over four glasses of port that he insisted were on the house and having delivered the drinks, backed away from the table obsequiously.

Henry raised his glass. "Here's to the two of you, you complete lifesavers." Then turning to Rick, "If it wasn't for your quick thinking, Phyllis may well have been seriously burnt, so thank you."

Phyllis looked adoringly at Rick. "I don't quite know what to say, but thank you so much Mr Donovan, it could all have been so very different." She then turned to Alicia. "And you, Sister, saved my Henry's life. How can I ever repay you?"

Henry Horsham cleared his throat. "Indeed, Sister Granger, I owe you my life." The table went quiet before Henry spoke again. "And I promise never to be a pain in the backside during ward rounds again!"

They all laughed at Henry's comment and downed the glasses of port.

"Whose birthday is it anyway?" Alicia asked.

"Henry's of course, and what a grand old age he has reached," Phyllis responded.

Henry cleared his throat with a touch of disapproval.

"Awww, just means he needs the love of a good woman to look after him." As Phyllis spoke, she grabbed Henry's hand and squeezed it, blowing him a kiss as she did so.

"Well, a very happy birthday to you, Mr Horsham," Alicia smiled at the old consultant.

"But I would avoid any more heart-shaped pieces of Turkish delight if I were you." Rick smirked, he just couldn't help himself. There was a slight moment of awkwardness before Henry saw the funny side and started to laugh.

It wasn't long before Rick and Alicia made their excuses, departed from the restaurant and made their way home. But not before they had said their goodbyes in *The Kafta and Kibbeh* to all and sundry. Asya had rushed up and without warning had kissed Rick goodbye, stating that if he ever needed a dance partner he knew where he could find her. His ego suitably massaged, Rick had been happy to note Alicia's look of disapproval. She clearly cared. Then there had been many handshakes before uncharacteristically Henry had insisted on giving everyone hugs goodbye. Rick thought to himself, *The old man has had too many ports or* Raki, *unless of course it was the Phyllis effect.* But then again it had been quite a night.

With the farewells done, Alicia and Rick walked hand in hand the short distance back to their respective houses, chatting as they ambled along.

"Well thank you for a fabulous if not momentous evening, Mr Donovan!" Alicia laughed and squeezed his hand as she did so.

"It was my absolute pleasure and you are right, the whole evening was great fun. If witnessing the human side of Henry Horsham isn't momentous, I am not sure what is!" Rick chuckled.

They arrived at Alicia's front door. She turned to face him.

"Rick, you said that there was something you

wanted to ask me tonight." She looked at him quizzically.

"Ah... yes. Well, I was wondering... well... um, are we an item?"

"Is that your way of asking me to be your girlfriend or partner or whatever it is these days?" She looked directly into his eyes.

Rick nodded. Alicia put her arms around him and whispered, "Yes, I would very much like that", and reaching up kissed him intimately.

CHAPTER 13

The days following the dinner date turned out to be very busy ones. Rick found himself on call two nights running when one of his colleagues had called in sick. He literally had no time to dwell on his romantic life. As well as working all day, he had carried out a number of emergency caesarean sections in the middle of the night, one for a diabetic woman who was as fat as a house with an equally enormous baby, the other for a pre-term triplet pregnancy in whom the mother had developed pre-eclampsia (a dangerous condition of pregnancy associated with very high blood pressure and potentially seizures). Fortunately, the outcome was happy for all concerned. The twelve-pound baby girl born to the portly lady required a temporary admission to the neonatal unit to settle her blood sugars. When placed adjacent to the tiny triplets, she resembled a miniature sumo wrestler. Fortunately she had the constitution of the aforementioned and was soon back on the ward guzzling at her mother's ample bosom. The triplets, after some initial breathing difficulties thrived and all concerned were delighted with the excellent care received courtesy of the NHS. Although he was quite literally knackered, Rick contemplated how much he loved his job.

It hadn't been much better for Alicia; the surgical ward was full to bursting and a number of the admissions had been quite unpalatable. A man who had apparently attended a bizarre sex party, had somehow managed to get a can of beer lodged up his anus. It had been one thing to put the fizzy drink up his arse, and quite another to take it out again. The good old NHS came to the rescue in the form of Mr Henry Horsham who took it upon himself to deliver a short sharp rebuke to the fellow concerned. Mr Horsham clearly indicated that he had better things to do than remove metal objects from the backside of an experimenting delinquent. Phyllis humoured him back into his previous good mood, but it was for all to wonder on the eccentricities of human nature.

Alicia had had to call an unsuspecting junior doctor to remove a retained tampon from another emergency admission. The item had been forgotten and was in residence for ten days, before the unfortunate woman's husband pointed out to his beloved that perhaps she needed a bath, such was the smell pervading the atmosphere around the luckless individual. Having removed the tampon, which by now supported an entire ecosystem of bacteria and fungi, and after performing a thorough douche of the good lady's nether regions, the patient in question was restored to her former glory. Although, she was in truth lucky not to have been seriously ill with *Toxic Shock Syndrome* which in some cases has been known to kill. Alicia had had to remove any wilted flowers and spray the whole ward with a complete can of air freshener, before the odour at least started to subside. The junior doctor who had done the honours, was unable to eat his lunch that day.

In the late afternoon, Rick had been called from his routine operating list to review a patient with a suspected ruptured ectopic pregnancy (pregnancy implanted outside the womb) who was bleeding to death internally. He had run the short distance to Bedlam ward in his operating hospital blues. Alicia had already inserted intravenous lines, ordered blood and noted that the patient's observations indicated life-threatening haemorrhage. Rick arrived, took one look at the patient and realising her impending mortality ordered her to be taken directly to the operating theatre. He and Alicia then helped the nursing auxiliary to push the trolley with the very pale, lifeless patient to the operating theatre. There simply hadn't been time to wait for the hospital porters. On arriving in theatre, the on-call anaesthetist put the patient to sleep whilst Rick scrubbed up ready for the woman's life-saving operation. Dressed in his hospital blues, Alicia couldn't help thinking how much she fancied the gynaecologist. He caught her eye, and winked. She smiled back, then left him to his work. They both knew that it never did any good to panic in circumstances like these, just a quiet and confident can-do attitude was what was required. The young patient lost her fallopian tube that day, but lived to tell the tale and the NHS had come up trumps again.

At the end of a very busy yet satisfying day, Rick finally arrived home. He was completely shattered. He grabbed a cold beer from the fridge, kicked off his shoes and gratefully reclined on his sofa. Alicia had already told him that she was doing a late shift and so would probably go straight home. Rick was grateful just to have finished his day and survived his horrendous on calls. So he finished his beer, then grabbing another one climbed wearily up the stairs, ran a bubble bath, removed his clothes and lay content in the watery suds.

The doorbell rang.

"Oh, sod it!" was Rick's only response, although the thought did cross his mind that perhaps Alicia had finished work early and had decided to call. Such ruminations injected a degree of energy back into his weary limbs. He clambered out of the bath, wrapped a towel around his midriff, and then with a naughty glint in his eye picked up the rubber duck from the side of the bath and charged down the stairs and flinging open the front door.

"Hi beautiful! Great to see..." Rick stopped in mid-sentence. He looked again at the woman standing in front of him and his heart missed a beat. This was an end to the day that he had not expected.

"Hello Rick." Belinda smiled and half giggled at his undressed state. "Why are you carrying a duck?"

"My god! I cannot believe it's you." Rick's mind raced back to the events of his recent past. Images of Enid, his old next-door neighbour and how he 'stole' her car in order to rush to the hospital in an emergency; how he had saved the life of a young woman that night who turned out to be Enid's niece, and how they had subsequently fallen for each other and then been forced to separate. And now that same ex-flame was here, at his front door… Belinda Jones. Rick just stood and gawped.

"Err… slightly awkward… um, Rick are you going to invite me in?" Belinda looked at him quizzically.

"Oh, I'm so sorry. Yes of course, please come in, come in. Forgive my manners." Rick stood aside and Belinda walked in. Closing the front door, Rick took a big breath. When they had first parted, it had taken him some time to get over her. She had been his patient, he had saved her life. Then they had fallen in love. Because she had been his patient, he had been warned that any romantic liaison was unethical. So after a long and painful deliberation, their joint decision had been to separate. The situation had broken both their hearts and fortunately they had never consummated their relationship; it would have made things doubly hard. Rick shook the cobwebs out of his head.

"Umm… Please go in, sit down. There is a beer in the fridge or a gin and tonic if you prefer. Help yourself. Forgive me while I just go and put some clothes on!" Rick scuttled upstairs.

Belinda shouted after him, "Don't get dressed on my account! I think you look rather cute."

Rick briefly hesitated, then continued on up the

stairs. He was a bag of mixed emotions. His heart jumped to see her again, and he fancied the pants off her, but there was some reluctance on account of his very strong feelings for Alicia. He dried off and dressed, then came down the stairs of his little terraced house to see her lounging on his sofa. She was dressed provocatively, in a short skirt that revealed a pair of long slim legs, a low-cut top that accentuated the line of her breasts, and a subtle hint of makeup that transformed her into someone who was very desirable. Certainly, she was not the same Belinda that he had parted with, not even a year ago. She seemed to have lost some of her previous naivety and her self-confidence was present in spades.

"I poured you a gin and tonic as well." She picked up the drink from the side table and passed it to him. He sat himself beside her. "Rick, it's so wonderful to see you. I have so missed you. You know, I have been thinking about this day for what seems like an eternity." She reached across and kissed him full on the lips.

Rick felt something of his old feelings towards her return and he responded to her kiss. "It's great to see you again too. It's just I can't quite believe you are here."

"Well, we agreed to a year's separation and I know it's not quite a year but pretty damn close. I just needed to see you again. Here's to us." Belinda raised her glass and emptied it. "May I help myself to another?"

"Sure." Rick watched her as she poured herself another drink. She sat down again, this time almost in his lap. He shifted over slightly then asked, "So what have you been up to over the last year?"

Undeterred, Belinda kicked off her sandals and settled into the cushions of the sofa, her silky legs tucked up under her. She took a sip from her newly refreshed G&T. "Well, to be honest after we decided to go our separate ways I was heartbroken. Aunt Enid was wonderfully supportive initially, but I had to just get away. Oh, by the way, thank you so much for looking after her when she had her stroke. She tells me that you still visit her in the retirement home and bring her flowers – you are a gorgeous softy!"

Rick nodded and smiled. "I'm very fond of the old girl. Anyhow, go on, finish the story – where did you go? What did you do?"

"Well to cut a long story short, I got a job on a cruise liner, as a cashier and accounts officer."

Rick's eyes widened. "Blimey, that's a bit different.

Good for you. No wonder we have seen neither sight nor sound of you. So where have you been on this cruise liner?"

"Mainly the Caribbean. Honestly Rick, whether it was exploring the mountains of St Lucia, or the volcanos of St Kitts, I had an absolutely fantastic time. Met a few *very* interesting individuals as well." She raised her eyebrows. The expression was full of innuendo which Rick was not quite sure he liked.

Sensing his disapproval, she quickly changed tack. "Anyhow, you can only take so much of swimming with dolphins, or sitting on a beautiful beach watching the sun go down after a Caribbean party."

"Blimey, sounds like paradise, I think I would have stayed on indefinitely!" Rick butted in.

"Well, after nearly a year of it, I had had enough. The company wanted me to stay on, but I refused to renew my contract. Rick, I wanted to get home and I wanted to see you." She leaned across and gently took his glass from him, then held his hand, her fingers slipping seductively over his. Her eyes searched his face and there was no mistaking her intent.

"Crikey, that's laying it on the table." Rick frantically searched his feelings. His loins stirred as Belinda's thigh brushed provocatively over his leg. He knew exactly what the physical side of him wanted. She leant towards him and kissed him with exquisite sensuality and his heart raced. She was no longer the naïve young woman whom he had saved in the operating theatre one year earlier and it was clear where this was going. As she gestured seductively towards him, her skirt moved up to reveal more of the sumptuous flesh of her thighs. Rick groaned, and his hand automatically reached across to touch her legs and the way she gasped at his touch heightened the physical tension between them. And then it happened.

A set of images flashed through his mind overcoming his by now considerable physical desires. Such imagery included mental pictures that were all of Alicia – her smile, her laugh, her caring for suffering patients, her crazy dancing, her dressed in hospital blues pushing patients to the operating theatre. Then images of the consequences of him sleeping with Belinda – the overwhelming feelings of hurt and betrayal. Needless to say, such ruminations were the trigger for an upright soldier to double over into a limp and rather sorry state. Rick withdrew his hand, now entirely sure of his feelings.

"I'm so sorry. Belinda, I just cannot do this. Forgive me."

She looked distraught. "No, I'm sorry Rick. Too much, too quickly." She immediately straightened herself out and sitting bolt upright pulled down her skirt to a more modest length. There was an awkward silence, before Belinda almost in tears spoke again. "There is someone else, isn't there?"

Rick took hold of her hand. "I'm so sorry Belinda, but… yes, there is… and as much as I want to tear off your clothes and ravage you… I just can't."

"Oh Rick, please don't say that. There hasn't been a day that I haven't thought about you. Wherever I was in the world and whoever I was with, just didn't compare. And it's not just because you saved my life and then were so wonderful to me and my Aunt Enid afterwards, it's just that I… I simply love you." She held his proffered hand and looked at him through watery eyes.

He looked at her tenderly, "Belinda… I am so sorry. But it would be a betrayal on my part to tell you anything different. Forgive me but I am in love with someone else. You are and always will be very dear to me but I cannot give you what you want."

She was openly crying now. "I should never have gone away. I knew in my heart of hearts that something like this would happen if I upped and left."

Her mascara was running and Rick took a tissue from his pocket and gently dried away her tears.

"Forgive me," Rick said quietly and took her in his arms and hugged her. They held each other for a few moments, then Belinda Jones pulled apart from him, stood up and straightened out her clothing. She was made of strong stuff and despite the obvious hurt that she felt, she was going to absorb it and soldier on.

After a few moments of silence, she spoke again. "Waste of time getting all dolled up for you, Mr Rick Donovan!" She smiled at him. He smiled back.

"Friends?" he ventured.

"Always," she countered.

Then still holding Rick's hand, Belinda Jones picked up her bag, and walked slowly to the front door of the little terraced house and exited. He followed her out into the small front courtyard and opened the front gate for her. She placed her arms around him once again and hugged him. He took her face gently in his hands and kissed her tenderly on the forehead. Then Belinda turned, walked away and never looked back.

*

It was midnight when Alicia finally went up to bed.

She had only been home for ten minutes or so as it had been a hell of a day, with her extra late shift turning into a nightmare and becoming a late, late shift. She heard her next-door neighbour's front door open and out of curiosity peeked through the closed bedroom curtain and out of her front window. Her heart missed a beat. Rick stood at his front gate hand in hand with a woman Alicia didn't recognise. Alicia watched as they embraced and continued almost in disbelief as Rick tenderly touched the young woman's face and kissed her, before she walked off into the night.

Alicia Granger withdrew from the window where she felt like an intruding voyeur. Feelings of hate, love, then sorrow all tormented her in an emotional rollercoaster. Many hours later when she finally drifted off into a disturbed slumber, it was the uneasy sleep of a young woman with a broken heart.

CHAPTER 14

The alarm on Rick's phone pounded his senses as it bleeped. He groaned, slapping the surface of the mobile to cease its early morning calls. Try as he might he could never hit the 'alarm off' area with any degree of accuracy in his blurry eyed state, and had to make do with the phone's 'snooze' facility. This was just as well since within a few minutes he was dozing off again. Ten minutes later the blasted thing restarted its sleep-depriving bleeps and this time, Rick forced himself awake.

He thought back over the events of the previous evening. *What a night. Crikey, that went to the wire, she could so easily have been lying next to me right now,* he thought to himself. Then with a slight pause, whispered, "And it would have buggered up everything."

He washed, dressed and then clambered down the

stairs for a light breakfast and a large mug of coffee. One thing that he knew though, was that after he had declined the hugely enticing offer of physical intimacy with Belinda, his feelings for Alicia must be pretty solid. Rick thought about how much Alicia meant to him and then how gorgeous she was. It was a beautiful morning and Rick stepped out of his own front door full of energy and confidence. He thought he would call on his next door neighbour just to say 'hi', before whizzing off to work.

He rang the doorbell. There was no answer. Perhaps she was still sleeping after a couple of late shifts, or perhaps she had already gone to work. "No matter, I'll catch up with her later," Rick said to himself matter-of-factly. He thought about the possibilities of sharing a glass or two of red wine with her later that evening; perhaps he could cook something for the two of them and then perhaps… His mind conjured up all sorts of more than pleasing images.

The gynaecologist walked in the bright sunshine to work. On his way through the park he whistled happily to himself and said a cheery 'hello' and 'good morning' to everyone he came across. Today was going to be a good day, or least that is what Rick thought. When he arrived at the hospital, he took the lift to the seventh floor and popped into to say 'hi' to his secretary Janice before dropping off his brief case into his own office. But for some strange reason, as he entered the secretaries' office, Janice didn't even look up at him but continued to type.

Rick persevered. "Hi Jan, lovely morning don't you think?"

This time his secretary momentary looked up, her eyes flitted from the work in front of her to briefly scowl at him before returning to the typing in hand. There was an almost imperceptible grunt, which was certainly not Janice's usual good morning greeting. Rick raised his eyebrows and assumed that she must be having a bad day. He repeated his greeting to the other secretaries in the office and for some reason they all seemed a bit hacked off with him too. Again, he got nothing but a series of grunts in reply to his cheery 'good morning, guys'. Perhaps they all were having a bad day, or perhaps there had been an argument among them, but for sure you could cut the atmosphere with a knife. Rick shook his head and was a little bewildered; he picked up his mail from Janice's desk (she would normally hand it to him with a beaming smile) and made his way to the door. As he went out, on closing the door behind him, he was sure that he heard a muffled, "Bastard!" and put his head back around the door to double check that the comment wasn't being directed at him. The secretaries in unison had their heads down and were all typing. Perhaps he had imagined it, but when he went to close the door behind him again, there was another muffled, "Shithead." Shaking his head in confusion, Rick left the secretaries to it and proceeded to his own office.

After checking his emails, Rick walked over to Bedlam ward to do a round and ensure all the emergency admissions and postoperative patients had been seen and managed appropriately. As he walked the short distance to the ward, a couple of the porters passed him in the corridor. The one whispered conspiratorially to the other, who laughed and then looking directly at Rick, appeared to wink at him. Thus far it was the strangest of mornings and Rick found that his previous good mood had started to evaporate.

Alicia had hardly slept at all. The vision of Rick canoodling with the young woman in the street just a few feet from her front door filled her with hurt, then sorrow, then finally anger. "How could he?" was the question that she asked herself over and over again. But there could be no doubt about it. The woman concerned was young and begrudgingly good looking, with a great pair of legs (*What a cow,* Alicia thought) and there could be no doubt that Rick had kissed and cuddled her in blazon view for the world to see. Alicia stopped herself. If he was having an affair with the cursed woman, wouldn't he be more discreet? Particularly when he was smooching with her right outside the house of the woman he just asked to be in a relationship with. It didn't make sense. Could she have been his sister? Or a cousin? Or just a friend that he knew especially well? Doubts started to cloud her mind, after all she had only ever known Rick Donovan to be a decent man. Her misgivings continued and she was almost giving him the benefit of the doubt at least until she arrived at work. The fact that she was so very upset made her realise the strength of her feelings for the scoundrel.

Since a restful night's sleep hadn't been an option, Alicia had been washed, dressed and out of the house at the crack of dawn. As she left for work, Rick's curtains were still closed. The fact that the 'tart', as Alicia now called her, hadn't stayed the night, bode well for Rick's defence. So when Alicia reached Bedlam ward she had almost convinced herself that there was a perfectly reasonable explanation for what she had witnessed the night before. At least until she saw Phyllis who was busy sorting out the notes for the morning ward rounds.

"Sister Granger… Alicia… you look awful.

Whatever is the matter?" Phyllis knew instinctively that something was very wrong with her friend and colleague. At that, Alicia burst into tears and was quickly ushered into the ward office where Phyllis had only a few weeks earlier been ravished by Henry Horsham — although the attempted ravishing was rudely interrupted, Phyllis smugly recalled that it had been successfully concluded in more appropriate surroundings later that day — and very nice it was too. Having sat her ward sister down, Phyllis looked anxiously down at her younger colleague. She looked mightily upset.

"Alicia, whatever is the matter?"

"Oh Phyllis…" With that, Alicia's tearful state went from a trickle to a gushing waterfall and Phyllis was very pleased that she had squirrelled her away into the relative privacy of the ward office.

"Go on," Phyllis gently encouraged.

"It's Rick… I think he's having an affair with someone else."

"The bastard, the bitch… I'll kill them both." Phyllis was not one to mince her words. A moment or two passed then taking a more conciliatory tone, Phyllis took Alicia by the hand and asked, "Are you absolutely sure, Alicia? Rick isn't really the philandering type."

"Well how do you explain him kissing and cuddling some tart outside his house at midnight last night?" Alicia looked up at her friend willing her to come up with a plausible explanation.

"Umm… that does sound somewhat suspicious, but… there may be some perfectly reasonable explanation." Phyllis looked doubtful and Alicia picked it up.

There was an urgent knock at the door.

"Go away!" Phyllis bellowed. But her admonishing tone was ignored and the door was pushed ajar. "Did you hear what I bloody well said? There really cannot be anything that urgent unless someone is dying out there."

"No, Phyllis, I need to get a grip." Alicia wiped away her tears and stood up. "Sorry… who is there and what is the matter?"

A red-faced staff nurse put her head around the door. "Sorry Sister but I thought you might like to know. The ward loudspeaker tannoy system is unfortunately on and for what it is worth, Mr Donovan doesn't seem like the type to have an affair!"

"Oh, bollocks! I mean… Oh God… this can't be

happening." With the door now open, Alicia could hear her voice reverberating around the ward. "Oh, bollocks!" could be heard from the reception desk to the far distant four bedded bay on Bedlam ward.

"Oh, fuck!" Alicia responded, grabbing her mouth the moment after she uttered the words.

"That isn't really helping, dear," Phyllis replied, turning off the tannoy system as she did so.

Mr Henry Horsham had arrived on the ward just in time to hear, "Oh, bollocks!" followed reasonably quickly by "Oh, fuck!" echoing from the Bedlam ward loudspeaker system. He was not impressed. The old general surgeon put his head around the ward office door with a look of extreme displeasure. He was about to open his mouth to give out the mother of all remonstrations when he saw Phyllis. She looked at him with her 'Not Now' stare and recognising distress in his ward sister, uncharacteristically withdrew from the scenario meek as a kitten. It appeared that Phyllis had well and truly tamed the old boy.

It took just another ten minutes for Alicia to put on her professional front and withdraw from the ward office. Initially she had been mortified that the Bedlam ward staff and patients alike now knew rather more than she would like about her personal life and had witnessed her more than fruity language. However, they all loved Sister Alicia Granger and as such were wonderfully understanding and supportive.

One elderly patient, Miss Ethel Smith, surprised Alicia at the end of Mr Horsham's ward round when she turned to Alicia and with a significant dose of vitriol came out with, "If I was you, Sister, I'd put the bastard's nuts in a vice and screw until he screams!"

Alicia replied with a raised eyebrow from Mr Horsham, "Umm… thank you, Miss Smith, I'll bear it in mind."

Hence when Mr Rick Donovan arrived on Bedlam to carry out his ward round, he was unaware that the entire population of patients and staff alike knew of his suspected infidelity. In fact since gossip travels fast in hospitals, the whole hospital was aware of the alleged illicit cavorting. That having been said, Rick wasn't blind to the fact that something was amiss – the secretaries were never uniformly miserable, and the porters never winked at him.

Rick was slightly later than usual pitching up to Bedlam ward. Knowing something was not quite right with the world, he wasn't altogether surprised with Phyllis's somewhat cold response to his enthusiastic greeting.

"Good morning, Phyllis." Rick beamed his broadest and most endearing smile.

"Is it?" The receptionist dumped his patient notes in front of him and abruptly turned, ignoring him. Rick was given the agency staff nurse to accompany him on his ward round and Sister Alicia Granger kept her distance at the far end of the ward. All very peculiar. When a young feminist patient gave him a filthy look and mumbled something about 'frigging men and their inability to keep their f-ing snakes contained within their f-ing trousers', Rick started to put two and two together.

Then Henry Horsham walked up to him with a serious look on his face. "Donovan," he said in the gravest tone, "I need to have a word with you."

Bloody hell, this really is serious, Rick thought to himself as he followed the senior consultant into the ward office like a naughty child, under the glare of what seemed like the entirety of the Bedlam ward staff.

"Now Mr Donovan, err… Rick, you seem to be unaware of the situation that has resulted from your… umm… indiscretion." The old consultant was having trouble finding his words. He felt like a father figure telling off his naughty child. He knew it was ridiculous. Henry had always maintained that people's private lives were their own business, and certainly after he had been discovered in that same office with his trousers nearly down, he was hardly one to lecture others. That having been said, actions that were deceitful and affected his staff and by extension his patients, needed to be challenged; anyhow, he had been put under pressure from Phyllis to say something to the cad. So he continued, "But I for one do not like my nurses, particularly the sister in charge of Bedlam, being upset in this way."

"Henry, what the hell are you talking about?" Rick was starting to get a bit hacked off with the shower of consistent negativity. "Everybody in this bloody hospital seems to have it in for me today. What on earth have I done? And come to think of it, what the hell business is it of yours?"

At that moment just to confound Rick's assertion that, *Everyone in this hospital seems to have it in for me*, there was a knock on the office door and a smiling staff nurse brought in two cups of coffee for the consultants as they talked. She then retreated with the word 'enjoy' and closed the door behind her. The staff nurse concerned had conspired with her colleagues about the best way to teach Rick a lesson and emptied a sachet of *Picolax* into Rick's coffee. The nurses had figured that if *Picolax* is used as a purgative to empty the most stubborn of constipated bowels, it should teach him a lesson that he would never forget. They were correct in this assertion and to add to his likely discomfort the resourceful nursing staff had locked the staff toilets on the ward and placed 'out of order' notices above their doors.

In a state of blissful ignorance and in the relative seclusion of the Bedlam ward office, with the loudspeaker tannoy system having being checked several times to ensure it was 'off' Rick explained the events of the previous night to Henry Horsham after hearing what he had been accused of. Henry, who clearly remembered the story of Belinda Jones, listened sympathetically to his colleague's account and then told Rick what had happened before he had arrived on the ward. Rick was mortified to learn how upset Alicia had been and the fact that his alleged affair had been broadcast to the entire hospital did nothing to lighten his mood, but at least it explained the bizarre behaviour of all his colleagues.

"Oh God, Rick, what a terrible misunderstanding. I knew that there would be a perfectly reasonable explanation," Henry lied.

"Henry, please, you have got to help me sort this out. No wonder everyone from the secretaries to

Phyllis have been acting strangely. Please talk to Phyllis and put the record straight. I have got to speak to Alicia and tell her the truth about this bloody mess." Rick drained the remainder of his coffee before getting up and heading for the door. The *Picolax* which has an onset of action of about 20 minutes, had started to have its initial effect, and Rick felt the first of many rumblings. He stopped in his tracks and without any warning, let rip. The fart surprised both gynaecologist and general surgeon. Henry raised an eyebrow but remained politely silent.

"Golly, many apologies, Henry. Not sure where that came from." Then it happened again. This time a long s-l-o-w trumpet and on this second occasion it was impossible to ignore.

"Bloody hell, Rick, what on earth is wrong with you? Were you on the curries last night or something?" Henry questioned.

It was then that Rick felt a sudden and desperate urge to empty his bowels. With his anal sphincter clamped for dear life, he rushed from the office and headed for the nearest staff toilet. It was the first time in living memory that both the staff loo doors were locked and makeshift signs hung above them with the words, 'Out of Order'. By now Rick had broken out into a sweat. His gut was rumbling audibly and he knew that it was only a matter of a few moments before an evacuation from his rear end would take place. In utter desperation, clinging on, he dashed to the patients' loos. They were all being utilised except one. An elderly and rather frail patient, Miss Dorothy Clatworthy, was speeding as fast as her Zimmer frame would allow towards the one remaining vacant lavatory. Without a word, Rick whizzed around the old girl into the loo and bolted the door behind him.

"Well really, how rude!" an indignant Miss Clatworthy exclaimed, but there was very little the old lady could do.

With seconds to spare and with huge relief, Rick reached his destination and the world then fell out of his bottom. As he sat on the lavatory throne, he breathed an enormous sigh of thanks for his safe delivery from what could have been an extremely embarrassing incident. However, the inexplicable and untimely nature of his urge to defecate, together with the locked staff loo that was supposedly 'Out of Order' raised his suspicions of foul play.

Rick Donovan, consultant gynaecologist, emerged from the female patient loo, weighing a good deal lighter than when he went in. Rick's mortification was further increased when a staff nurse with a grimace on her face, proceeded to spray the immediate vicinity with air freshener to counter the malodourous whiffs emanating from patient's toilet.

Miss Dorothy Clatworthy, seeking retribution for the interruption of her planned ablutions, added to his discomfort by declaring, "My goodness, Mr Donovan, I think you need to see a doctor, preferably one that deals with ailments of the bowels!"

Rick had had enough. With a determined look on his face he strode purposefully back into the ward office and grabbed the microphone for the Bedlam ward tannoy system. He hesitated for just a second or two, his finger hovering on the broadcast button. Then Rick considered the car crash that had been his morning thus far and his only thought then was, *Bollocks to this, I'm going to clear up this nonsense once and for all. He* pressed the microphone's broadcast button:

"Would all staff, other than those on essential duty, please report to the ward office. I repeat, please would all members of staff report immediately to the ward office!" The announcement reverberated around Bedlam and its formality and urgency surprised the nurses, domestics, and receptionist. In particular the gaggle of nurses who had planned the *Picolax* assault suddenly looked worried. Assembling the entire staff from the ward into the office proved to be challenging, not because people had failed to respond but because of the diminutive size of the office. With the room packed full, and overflowing out into the main ward, Rick cleared his throat and started.

"Since my arrival this morning in this hospital and subsequently onto this ward, I have been ignored, insulted and finally poisoned." Rick paused for effect, then continued in the sternest voice he could muster, "This is not acceptable behaviour, particularly when those accountable for making my life miserable have made assumptions that are just NOT true." Rick paused again, then restarted. "In particular the lacing of a person's drink, coffee in my case, with medication taken from this ward without that person's knowledge is a serious offence, if not a crime."

By now there were nervous mutterings among the staff. The nurses and indeed Phyllis who had orchestrated and then been responsible for the laxative in Rick's coffee stood at the back of the ensemble looking very sheepish and slightly worried. Alicia stood slightly further forward and just looked directly at Rick, her eyes never straying from his face.

He continued, "However, I suspect the reason for

this unacceptable behaviour was secondary to the high regard you all have for our current ward sister, Sister Alicia Granger, and the incorrect speculation that I had done the dirty on her."

A few disapproving mutterings went around the room before quiet returned. As well as the staff from Bedlam ward, patients particularly those who had heard Alicia's previous unintended tannoy outburst had started to gather to listen to what the guilty bastard had to say.

Rick continued, "Some of you may remember a young woman who was admitted here onto this ward about a year ago. I cannot tell you her name because of confidentiality issues, but I can say that she was seriously ill and very nearly died. The night she was admitted I was on call from home and rushed in to perform emergency surgery. Getting into the hospital that night was interesting and involved borrowing my next-door neighbour's car, being followed by the cops and subsequently getting nicked or at least ending up in police custody – but that's another whole story and one from which I may say I was completely exonerated!" Rick stopped as the events of that night ruminated around his mind. He looked around at those gathered in front of him. All eyes were focused on the gynaecologist, from Henry Horsham who well remembered his colleague's previous traumatic brush with the authorities, to the ward cleaner, who stood open-mouthed waiting for the end of the story.

The silent pause was broken by Miss Dorothy Clatworthy, who now having seen to her ablutions, had now gathered with some of the other patients behind the assembled staff. "Do carry on, Mr Donovan, we are all ears!" she shrieked.

"Thank you, Miss Clatworthy." Rick knew the old girl well. She had been admitted with a third-degree prolapse such that her womb had hung between her legs, and her gait, despite her Zimmer, resembled an elderly cowboy with severe piles. She had made a good postoperative recovery following her vaginal hysterectomy and now stood unimpaired listening intently to her surgeon. She seemed to have already forgiven Rick for beating her to the bathroom when he had been so clearly in urgent need of its use.

Rick nodded to the old lady. "Oh, and sorry for commandeering the loo just now, but I was about to explode, courtesy of my colleagues here who I believe spiked my coffee. But anyway enough of that." Another pause followed as Rick gathered his thoughts. "Now going back to the young woman whose life this hospital saved. Following her recovery and rehabilitation, I became very close to her but will add that nothing inappropriate occurred." Rick took a deep breath in. "However, it was a relationship that could never take place. The General Medical Council looks dimly on such relationships and indeed as a general rule there is a code of conduct which prohibits any such liaison, however genuine." Rick looked ever so slightly upset as he spoke and the gathered medical team as well as patients had even started to feel a bit sorry for him.

Then looking directly at Alicia, Rick spoke quietly and from the heart. "Anyhow, we agreed that any relationship was impossible and she moved away and I don't mind telling you that it was hugely upsetting for everyone concerned. I hadn't seen her for a year, until last night when the same young lady visited my home completely out of the blue. It was great to see her. We laughed and reminisced over a glass of wine or two and it was wonderful to hear that she is doing really well and her life is good. I can also say that absolutely *nothing* inappropriate occurred. When she left my house at around midnight, it is true that we hugged. Hugged as good friends might hug. I kissed her goodbye as a dear friend. I know that she wanted to rekindle things, but I couldn't. And I couldn't because I am in love with someone else. That someone else just happens to be Sister Alicia Granger." Rick bowed his head.

Alicia stood dumbfounded after Rick's little speech; the fears and doubts tumbled away and to a cheering ensemble of ward staff and patients, she rushed up and threw her arms around him. Phyllis wept, and even old Henry Horsham had a tear in his eye.

"I'm so sorry for doubting you," Alicia whispered into his ear. "Trouble is… I think I am falling in love with you too."

Rick gently took her face in his hands and kissed her tenderly, much to the delight of those gathered around. Then the applause of their audience continued, Rick abruptly pulled away with a concerned look on his face. "So sorry, be back in a minute; excuse me everybody, needs must and all that." Rick ran through his startled colleagues and patients, heading directly for the staff toilets, the inevitable consequence of his spiked coffee.

CHAPTER 15

The invitations for the big wedding day had been sent out only six weeks earlier. Dick and Joyce had decided that they were not going to wait for months and months to tie the knot. They both knew and looked forward to the rest of their lives together and now wanted to make it official.

The wedding banns had been proclaimed at the proposed venue, which was St Mary's Anglican Church. The vicar was an elderly, Scottish, bespectacled and slightly deaf ex-military padre by the name of Hamish Dower. He had been a close friend of Dick's and the two of them had served in the Her Majesty's Armed Forces together, many years previously. Hamish was an interesting character having previously served as a veteran paratrooper and then a member of the elite SAS, with an exemplary military record and a previous youthful propensity for violence. Following a flying accident, in which Hamish was lucky to survive, there came his calling from God, who reached Hamish via the attention of a buxom German nun called Sister Magda Manfried. Her attention led him to a religious conversion and then vocation to the Anglican priesthood. Almost overnight Hamish went from an efficient killing machine to a saviour of souls, from a soldier in one of the most elite fighting forces in the world to Army Chaplain. To say that he had the respect of his men and could match them in the bar or indeed the battlefield was an understatement. Hamish was worldly wise and hard as nails, but with a good heart and real sense of justice. The passing of years had done nothing to tame his fiery personality, or indeed appetite for voluptuous women, although now on the verge of early dementia, his memory often failed him. Hamish was, to say the least, quite a character, and Dick was very fond of his old comrade, not least because during their military service Hamish had saved Dick's life:

*

It was 1994 and despite the fall of the Soviet Union and the lifting of the Iron Curtain, a frosty relationship still existed between the West and Russia. A much younger Major Hamish Dower had been sent on detachment to a frontline RAF flying station, called RAF Bruggen, which was located just across the Dutch border in Germany. He had been posted as a liaison officer between the British Military and their German hosts prior to the forthcoming NATO exercises. Joint military manoeuvres when British, German, American, Dutch and Italian armed Forces all got together to mimic beating the hell out of each other, needed a fair bit of co-ordination. Such exercises were carried out with each side taking it in turns to be the enemy (invariably the enemy was described as the nasty Russian Bastards), who much to the delight of the co-ordinated NATO forces invariably took a hammering. Hamish himself managed to dish out a few thrashings in bar brawls to disgruntled foreign militia who took exception to being whipped in drinking games, although he was never any good at card games, particularly poker.

It was at such a poker game that Major Hamish Dower and Flight Lieutenant Dick Chambers met one late afternoon in the Officers' Mess bar at RAF Bruggen. Dick had just returned from a successful flying sortie and needed a beer; Hamish was thirsty after begrudgingly spending three long hours discussing the preliminary planning for the next joint international exercise with the Krauts, Cloggies and

Ities. When enough beer had been consumed to render most mortals unconscious, the poker had begun. The forfeit for the unfortunate loser had been to strip stark bollock naked and run a lap around the Mess with only a hat on. Hamish, although victorious in the beer race fared less well in the poker game in which Dick was triumphant. In defeat, Hamish had been true to his word and having stripped to his birthday suit, jogged around the Officers' Mess adorned only in his beret.

It had been unfortunate that during his naked run, Hamish had been met by the somewhat prudish Station Commander who had been showing around some German dignitaries prior to a private dinner at the Station Commander's residence in the hope of more cordial relations between the British Military and the local townsfolk. On meeting the startled delegation, Hamish in proper military fashion came to an abrupt halt before standing to attention and saluting his senior officer. The head of the small delegation, who also happened to be the local Mayoress, Fraulein Zelda Schmidt, admirably took it upon herself to diffuse the situation. On looking down to Hamish's nether regions, she congratulated him on having a 'very fine Bratwurst', to which Hamish replied, "Thank you, ma'am," before continuing with his naturist jog.

Major Hamish Dower was later severely reprimanded by an irate Station Commander, although relations with the locals seemed to reach a new high, especially after Hamish had responded positively to Fraulein Schmidt's invitation to dinner and at her request had promptly shagged her.

Following these shenanigans, Hamish and Dick had become great friends, although even Dick had to admit Hamish remained a bit of a rebellious loose cannon. But this was about to change when Hamish asked Dick for the unique experience of a ride in one of Her Majesty's Tornado fighter jets. In view of the fact that Hamish was a liaison officer, which meant that he also bridged the gap between the different Forces within the British Military, Dick thought that his request was entirely reasonable as did his Squadron Commander. So in the summer of 1994, Flight Lieutenant Dick Chambers took to the skies with Major Hamish Dower in the navigator seat. Preceding his flight, Hamish of course had undergone some basic Tornado flight training and so became familiar with potential emergency procedures, but this was the first time he had ever experienced fast jet flying and he loved it. Dick had shown his friend the fantastic versatility of his flying machine and together they explored the local area from the air. Germany was beautiful, with its lakes, forests, rivers and stunning villages. Dick also flew over a couple of naturist camps where some red-faced fat German men waved their fists, while in contrast a number of naked blonde beauties waved excitedly. Dick's only comment into his radio headset to his colleague sitting in the rear seat was, "If you ever fancy another game of poker!"

Hamish's maiden flight continued and all seemed well, but then disaster struck. On the final approach to landing back at RAF Bruggen, a *bird strike* occurred. Such collisions between birds and aircraft were known to occur, particularly when landing or taking off, and there had been cases of fatalities. It was, however, completely unexpected when the solitary bird hit Dick's Tornado canopy head-on, smashing the reinforced acrylic plastic and impacting directly into his head. Dick's flying helmet saved him from sure death, but the impact rendered the aviator unconscious.

As the Tornado spiralled out of control, Hamish shrieked into his mouthpiece, "Mayday! Mayday! Bird strike! Pilot not responding! What the f**k do I do now?!"

The Tower could see the Tornado uncontrollably flying off and descending rapidly, but fortunately on a trajectory away from the built-up, populated areas of the adjacent town and into rural woodland. The traffic controllers breathed a sigh of relief that at least the risk of major population fatalities were now minimised. With an unconscious or dead pilot, there was no other course of action open to them and the radio advice to Hamish had been loud and clear, "Eject, eject!"

Hamish didn't need telling twice. His brief safety training, carried out just before the flight, automatically directed him and he pulled the ejection seat lever. He knew this particular system meant that both pilot and navigator would be ejected simultaneously. The cartridges fired and miniature rockets propelled Dick and Hamish high above the flailing aircraft before their respective parachutes opened and they slowly descended back towards the earth. Hamish saw the stricken Tornado impact the ground with an enormous explosion, but fortunately it was in a forested area and Hamish calculated a likely zero body count. He turned towards his friend in the sky and could see that his head was still slumped and he remained either unconscious or dead. They were both descending into the middle of large lake and it was only a matter of seconds before they both hit the water.

Hamish uncoupled his harness in the air, some ten feet from the surface of the lake so that directly on impact with the water he could swim with all his strength towards his friend whose head was now below the water line. Hamish reached his friend in record time and somehow uncoupled Dick from his parachute, lifted his head above the gentle waves of the inland lake and swam with a life saver's determination towards dry land. As he swam he swallowed and inhaled water that splashed up against his face and so his strength dwindled and he became weaker and weaker. The shoreline was so close and Hamish had been so exhausted, it would have been so easy for him to release his friend to his fate and save himself. But this had never been in the SAS man's character or thoughts. They either make it together or they both die. Hamish lost consciousness a few feet from terra firma, but seconds before he succumbed to the inevitable, he saw what he thought were two giant penguins running down the lakeside beach and into the water towards him and Dick.

Sister Magna Manfried and Sister Winifred Muller were dressed in their black and white nun habits, strolling together along the shore of the lake not far from their convent. They had been reciting their rosaries and praying to the Blessed Virgin when they had witnessed the two men parachuting out of the sky and into the lake. It was obvious that the men were in trouble, and the nuns hoicked up their habits and ran down to the water's edge, before plunging into the lake to drag both unconscious men up onto the shore. Once on dry land, Sister Magna removed their respective helmets and checked them in turn for their breathing and pulse – she found none. She shouted at her fellow nun to start mouth-to-mouth resuscitation, but Sister Winifred had panicked, having never been exposed to a member of the opposite sex before, and ran off to get help. So Sister Magna lined the two men up and whilst simultaneously praying to her god for help, carried out alternate mouth-to-mouth resuscitation first on Dick, then on Hamish.

Dick was the first to respond; coughing and spluttering, he must have expelled half his body weight in the inhaled water. His head hurt, he was cold and wet, but he could still feel his fingers and toes and was able to move all four of his limbs. He vaguely remembered the last few moments before the bird strike and was sufficiently aware to realise that they must have ejected. He looked over to where his friend lay with a nun leant over him, breathing into his watery lungs. He saw Sister Magna breathe into his friend again and again before finally she stopped and then calmly laying her hands on his chest she started to pray, before rolling her hands together and pushing onto his chest wall. Almost miraculously, Hamish opened his eyes before he too expelled the copious quantities of fluid that had been trapped inside his lungs.

Hamish returned from the clutches of death, opened his eyes with a start and momentarily looked into the blue eyes of his saviour. In one spark of a lifetime, he looked deep into the soul of the woman he would love forever – her love, her compassion, her selflessness, her wonderful sense of fun and then her profound closeness to an all-powerful and ever loving deity. In that moment Hamish experienced a glimpse of eternity, a revelation of God, and his life was changed forever.

In the days and weeks that followed, Flight Lieutenant Dick Chambers acknowledged that his friend and comrade had saved his life that day, firstly by carrying out the correct procedures for them both to eject, and secondly by preventing him from drowning, albeit with the help of a German nun. The detailed Accident Investigation that took place thereafter, conceded that Dick had NOT been negligent as a pilot and the accident had been a freak of nature. Dick was completely exonerated and in time returned to his flying duties as a Squadron Leader. The Investigation Report further concluded that Major Hamish Dower had acted gallantly and indeed had saved the life of his pilot. He was decorated for his bravery and wore the award with pride knowing that he had saved his friend's life.

Following the accident Hamish was restless, he had for the first time in his life really come across something quite extraordinary. He tried in vain to contact Sister Magna Manfried, but to no avail. He wrote to her explaining what he had experienced that day beside the lake, and the revelation that it induced. She thwarted his attempts to see her and stopped all communication save for one last letter in which she explained what Hamish had experienced and how he should now conduct his life. Unlike so many of the clergy that Hamish had come across, here at last in a relatively remote German convent, was a person with a true vocation and a real channel of God's love. Many years later Sister Magna's letter still remained Reverend Hamish Dower's most prized possession.

Dear Major Hamish

As I write to you please forgive my bad English, but I will do my very best to explain to you with God's guidance what happened on that day in the summer. At the time both you and your friend were drowning in the lake, God had willed that Sister Muller and me were praying close to the water's edge, and it was of course our Christian duty to save you, but it was directed by our Lord. I thank you for your letters that told me of deep feelings of love that you had experienced when our eyes met. But Hamish, the glimpse of what you experienced was not of the flesh and was not of love for me as a human being or a woman. What you experienced for a brief moment in time was the infinite love and care of our God. I believe God reached you through me and showed you a tiny part of his truth. It is very rare to be blessed with such a revelation, but it means that you now have great responsibility to carry out his blessed will. If what you experienced is real to you, you must now follow a different path, a path of enlightened love, of justice and of service to our God.

Bless you very specially Hamish Dower.

With love in the Lord's name

Sister Magna Manfried

The day after he received the letter, Major Hamish Dower resigned from any future active combat duties and successfully applied for the Anglican priesthood. Three years later, the *Reverend* Hamish Dower was made a chaplain in the British Armed Forces. He was true to his vocation and proved to be a very effective padre and witness to God's love and justice. He never again resorted to violence unless it was in the defence of others, but admittedly retained a weakness for women and ale. Hamish never lost contact with his old friend Dick Chambers and so despite the many years that had passed by, he was absolutely delighted to be asked to officiate at Dick and Joyce's wedding.

CHAPTER 16

As well as St Mary's Anglican Church being the ideal location for Dick and Joyce's wedding ceremony, the adjoining church hall was the perfect venue for the reception. Joyce had made it her mission to decorate the little hall so that it resembled a feast of floral colour and gaiety. Joyce's friends and acquaintances in the WRVS had been mobilised and the old girls had transformed a bland church hall into a wonderful wedding location. Each of the little round tables was adorned with an array of beautifully cut flowers, with every tablecloth and seat cushion embroidered with a '*D&J*' logo. Joyce had looked at the cost of wedding caterers and having been shocked at the exorbitant prices they charged for a mediocre wedding banquet, decided the girls from the WRVS could do the job better for half the price. And so the little church hall kitchen had witnessed a new lease of life with a flurry of activity not seen since the Archbishop of Canterbury had visited the parish and called in for afternoon tea many years earlier.

The WRVS under Joyce's stern but kindly leadership also managed to clean, polish and decorate St Mary's, so that it looked like a renovation project. Hamish Dower was chuffed to bits to see his little church undergoing such a transformation. He delighted in the company of a number of buxom widows who were not too old to blush at the old padre's thinly disguised innuendos. But more than that, the entire community appeared to be involved in what was going to be a very special occasion.

When Rick and Alicia had received their wedding invitations they had been doubly delighted. The news of Dick and Joyce's forthcoming nuptials was one reason to celebrate, but the letter contained within the invitation card had quite touched them. On the day that they had received the invitation, the two of them had been sitting in Rick's back garden with a cup of coffee each. On opening the envelope that had been addressed to both of them, a letter in Joyce's handwriting, but signed by both her and Dick, dropped out. Rick had read out loud the letter contained therein and both he and Alicia had been completely bowled over by its content.

Dear Rick and Alicia

We would be so delighted if you could come to our wedding to witness and celebrate our joining together into the married state. You have both been outstanding friends to us, the like of which words are not sufficient to convey.

Rick, for your part you have saved both of our lives. Firstly by a magnificent rugby tackle on the seventh floor of the hospital on my soon-to-be husband, and then by your wonderful clinical and surgical skills in treating and curing my cancer.

Alicia, you are the most wonderful ward sister. Your care of me before and after my recent operation was exemplary. I do not know what I would have done without you. I also know that following my retirement Bedlam Ward is now in the safest of hands. You have become a trusted friend and as such it would give me great pleasure if you would consent to be a bridesmaid on my wedding day.

Rick, I don't know quite how to ask you this, but we would be both be truly honoured if you would walk me down the aisle on the day itself. You have become part of our lives and if it were not for you neither of us would be here now. You would do us a great honour to accept this role.

Yours fondly,

Dick and Joyce

Alicia had immediately written back, thanking them

and accepting the kind invitation, and stating that Rick would be flattered to walk Joyce down the aisle, and she of course would be honoured to be a bridesmaid. Joyce's letter had quite touched them both.

On the morning of the wedding, the sun was shining as the pews of St Mary's Church started to fill with wedding guests. Hamish had instructed the church bells to be rung for at least half an hour before the congregation had arrived and to stop the moment that the bride was seen at the back of the church. The motley crew of bell ringers were knackered having been practising their trade every day for the last two weeks to build up their muscles and stamina for the forthcoming marathon event – and now they took pride in the wonderful sound generated from the church tower. It wasn't long before the little church was filled to capacity with well-meaning guests. Dick was standing nervously with his best man, another ex-military chum who had been given rather unusual instructions with regard to the presentation of the wedding rings. The back doors of the church opened and the bell ringing came to a halt as Mrs Florence Forbes, a long-term churchgoer and ardent WRVS member, fired up the old church organ and smiled to herself as she hit the keys to 'The Wedding March'. Joyce, resplendent in a demure ivory wedding skirt and jacket, complete with a broad-rimmed hat with French veil and silk ribbon, beamed as she and Rick slowly walked down the aisle towards her beloved Dick.

The Reverend Hamish Dower stood on the steps of the altar of St Mary's tapping his foot to the bashed out notes of 'The Wedding March' smiling first at Joyce and then, looking towards his old friend who stood waiting for his bride, winked and mouthed, "She looks a cracker!" When they reached the altar, Joyce released Rick's arm and took the hands of her husband-to-be. Her face was radiant with joy as she turned to face him.

"You look beautiful," was all Dick could whisper before the two of them turned frontward to face Hamish.

"Dearly beloved, we are gathered here in God's house, to witness the joining of Joyce Evans and Dick Chambers in holy matrimony… and may I say, Dick, how gorgeous your beloved looks." A few titters could be heard and one or two eyebrows were raised in the congregation before the old Scottish vicar continued, "And may I also say how welcome you all are to the parish of St Mary's, especially the lovely ladies of the WRVS." At this the organist, Miss Florence Forbes, blushed as the vicar's eyes looked up at her and then he winked.

The old vicar hesitated and then appeared to be momentarily confused; he looked down at his prayer book and then asked, "Who gives this woman to be this man's wife?" Hamish stuttered.

Oh God, the old boy has moved forward to the middle of the service and we haven't even started yet, Rick thought to himself, but there was nothing for it. "I do." Rick tried to sound solemn, but it just didn't seem to fit.

"Umm, and I believe, young man, that not only are you giving away Miss Evans, but have been instrumental in saving her life. It seems most fitting then that you are giving her away."

"Err, yes…" Rick wasn't quite sure what to say. He returned to his seat next to Alicia on the front phew. The old vicar carried on.

"The words I shall now speak are from the Book of Common Prayer." There was a brief pause before he took a deep breath and then continued. He knew the words like the back of his hand. *"Matrimony is an honourable estate, instituted of God in the time of man's innocency signifying unto us the mystical union that is betwixt Christ and his Church; which holy estate Christ adorned and beautified with his presence…"*

In the front row Rick's mind wondered at the

occasion. He was so chuffed for Dick and Joyce; it had been quite a journey to where they now stood together. It had, to say the least, been a hugely traumatic year for both of them, but now here they were both beaming with happiness and about to make their vows to each other.

"*...to satisfy men's carnal lusts and appetites, like brute beasts that have no understanding...*"

Rick took Alicia's hand and softly whispered, "I should be so lucky!"

"Rick Donovan, control yourself," Alicia whispered back and squeezed his hand.

As Hamish continued his monologue "*...but reverently, discreetly, advisedly, soberly, and in the fear of God; duly considering the causes for which Matrimony was ordained...*"

Alicia turned discreetly to Rick. "Now that's more like it, particularly soberly for you!" They both chuckled and Rick felt a wonderful union with the woman standing next to him.

"*...if any man do allege and declare any impediment, why they may not be coupled together in Matrimony...*" Hamish waited for effect as the whole congregation held their breath. Rick looked around at the assembled flock and he felt a flutter in his chest. Towards the back of the church a distinguished-looking old man had just entered and seated himself. With him and firmly clutched to his arm was a stunning blonde at least 30 years his junior. The two men's gaze met and Rick was delighted to see his old boss, Sir John Rawarse, looking so well and happy, if not a little more rotund than when Rick last saw him. He had obviously taken time out from his French vineyard and travelled back to *Blighty*, not wanting to miss his old ward sister's wedding. Rick turned once again to face the front.

"Will you have this woman to be your lawful wedded wife, to live together after God's ordinance in the holy estate of Matrimony? Will you love her, comfort her, honour, and keep her, in sickness and in health; and, forsaking all other, keep only unto her, so long as you both shall live?"

Dick turned to Joyce with a clear mind, sincere heart and joy in his response, "I will."

"Will you have this man to be your wedded husband, to live together after God's ordinance in the holy estate of Matrimony? Will you love, honour, and keep him, in sickness and in health; and, forsaking all other, keep only unto him, so long as you both shall live?"

It was Joyce's turn to respond and she said it with bursting happiness. "I will."

Rick noticed that the old ward sister had not

agreed to 'serve and obey him'. He whispered seriously into Alicia's ear, "What happened to serve and obey? I hope you wouldn't miss that out if you ever married me."

Alicia whispered back, "You've got NO chance!" But her heart missed a beat at such a suggestion.

Hamish cleared his throat. "We will now have the exchanging of the rings, and there will be a slight delay in the proceedings." There were murmurs in the congregation as Dick's best man left his side and disappeared into the vestry, before reappearing moments later with a cute little Jack Russell puppy, complete with collar and attached pouch containing the rings.

"I know that this is somewhat unconventional," Hamish uttered, and then turning to Joyce, "but Dick wanted to do this for you."

The puppy scampered directly up to Joyce wagging his diminutive tail, stopped at her feet and looked up. She promptly burst into tears and scooped up the little ball of fluff and cradled him in her arms. There were utterings of surprise from the congregation at such goings on within the Lord's house. However the general consensus was one of delight for they all knew how much Joyce's previous pooch, Geoffrey, had meant to her, and this little dog was the spit of her old companion.

Joyce turned to Dick. "You absolute darling. What a wonderful surprise on our wedding day." She knew straightaway what she was going to call this new and wonderful addition to her life. "I shall call him Hamish Junior in honour of you, Vicar." She leant towards Dick to kiss him as the Reverend Hamish Dower, who was not overly flattered by the use of his name for a Jack Russell, looked on.

With that, the best man opened the little pouch attached to the puppy's collar and took out two sparkling wedding rings and handed them to Hamish.

"Who giveth this woman to be married to this man? Oops, sorry. I think we have already done that bit. That was you, wasn't it Rick?"

"Indeed Vicar, I think Dick probably needs to take hold of Joyce's right hand," Rick responded from the front row to titters from the congregation.

"Ah, yes indeed, indeed yes. Ah, thank you Rick." Hamish found his place in the common prayer book again, then looking at Dick instructed him to take Joyce's right hand. "My friend, say after me… *I, Dick Chambers…*"

Dick repeated the words that his old comrade

spoke looking directly at Joyce and with the sincerest heart. *"I take you, Joyce Evans, to be my wedded wife, to have and to hold from this day forward, for better for worse, for richer, for poorer, in sickness and in health."* There was a pause and Dick added, "I think we've already lived through that bit!" Before continuing, *"To love and to cherish, till death us do part, according to God's holy ordinance."* He affectionately squeezed her hand.

It was then Joyce's turn and she repeated after Hamish, *"I, Joyce Evans, take you my darling Dick to be my wedded husband, to have and to hold from this day forward, for better for worse, for richer, for poorer, in sickness and in health, to love, cherish, BUT NOT TO OBEY, till death us do part, according to God's holy ordinance; and thereto I give thee my troth."* They chuckled with the congregation and the Reverend Dower at her declining to obey her beloved.

Hamish lay the two rings in the fold of his prayer book. Then holding the book with one hand gently took his canine namesake from Joyce and tucked him under his arm. He instructed Joyce and Dick to each take a ring and repeat after him. *"WITH this ring I thee wed, with my body I thee worship, and with all my worldly goods I thee endow: In the Name of the Father, and of the Son, and of the Holy Ghost. Amen."*

Then a smiling Reverend Hamish Dower joined

their hands together and spoke out in a booming voice, *"Those whom God hath joined together let no man put asunder.* I now pronounce you man and wife. You may kiss the bride."

Dick took Joyce into his arms and kissed her tenderly to the delight and cheers of the assembled congregation. The excitement of it all was too much for the little Jack Russell puppy who had yet to perfect his house training habits. The Reverend felt a warm flow trickle down his cassock. He gently lifted the whimpering puppy with both hands and whispered, "It's all right, old chap, my waterworks aren't always that well behaved either."

CHAPTER 17

St Mary's church hall was a throng of laughing, fun-
loving, and thoroughly decent folk. It was more
action than the old place had seen for many years
past. Joyce together with her WRVS colleagues and
friends had done a wonderful job in the decoration
and catering. Each guest was warmly greeted by the
newlyweds and handed a generous glass of Prosecco
as they came into the hall. The place was full of
laughter, hugs and kisses. Most of the nursing staff
(with their respective partners) from Bedlam ward
had been invited. Phyllis and Henry Horsham, the
entire WRVS and much to Reverend Hamish
Dower's delight, Florence Forbes, who continued a
lively repertoire of music on an old upright piano as
guests flooded into the hall. A number of Dick's old
comrades which included his best man, Ron
Arkwright were the same in number as the bride's

bunch of friends and acquaintances, and no less vocal. Indeed, a couple of the old soldiers, including Ron himself, were soon charming the ladies of the WRVS, as well as the nurses from Bedlam.

Sir John Rawarse, together with his young and rather beautiful wife had supplied all the wine, from their own vineyard, as a wedding present to his old ward sister. The Reverend Hamish Dower, having recently changed out of his pee-soaked cassock into an open-necked shirt minus the dog collar, stood chatting animatedly to Sir John whilst taking full advantage of the abundant cases of the most wonderful red wine. Rick and Alicia stood with them and so Rick had taken the opportunity to introduce Alicia to his old boss, who in turn introduced his new wife to all concerned. All of them couldn't help noticing Hamish intermittently stealing sneaky glances at Florence as she concentrated on bringing the old piano back to life, with a fabulous rendition of *'At Last'*. She really was quite a pianist. Every now and again, Florence would look up from the keyboard and return the clergyman a big smile. Hamish couldn't believe it, but to his amazement he found himself being a little bashful and blushing!

It was two o'clock in the afternoon when they all sat down to eat. A number of the younger WRVS ladies had agreed to act as waitresses for the occasion and now busily scuttled backwards and forwards between the hall and the kitchen. At the head table Dick and Joyce sat grinning at their friends and colleagues; Rick and Alicia sat to one side of them with Hamish Dower. Seated on the other side was the best man Ron Arkwright, with Sir John and Mrs Rawarse. Hamish Junior now lay exhausted and sound asleep in a 'Doggie' bed by Joyce's feet. His new mistress was so happy she felt her heart would burst with joy.

Everyone agreed that the wedding menu was fantastic and the WRVS had done Joyce and Dick proud. They started with a *roasted parsnip and apple soup with baby herb croutons*, followed by *chicken supreme with roasted root vegetables and scalloped potatoes,* all topped off with *honey and vanilla cheesecake and lashings of fresh cream.* Three bottles of delightful red wine from Rawarse Vineyards were placed on each table and were devoured, leading to high spirits. There was tomfoolery and laughter in buckets, with animated chatter and a wonderful sense of bonhomie. The wedding party finished their desserts as the best man, Ron, stood up to begin his speech.

"Friends, I am honoured to stand here today by the side of my dearest old pal, Squadron Leader Dick Chambers, on the occasion of his union with his delightful and dare I say it… rather good-looking wife, Joyce or Mrs Joyce Chambers as I should now address you." Ron gave her the slightest of ingratiating nods as a ripple of chortles spread around the hall.

"Hands off, mate," Dick playfully jested.

Ron continued, "You will note, the two of them already have an addition to the family…"

"You old scoundrel, Dick," another one of Dick's former RAF friends blurted out with undisguised innuendo.

"I meant in the form of Hamish Junior. No offence, Padre. This delightful little chap who lies fast asleep in his doggie bed at his new mistress's feet."

"He's only fallen asleep since your speech started." More chuckles from the wedding guests.

"I'll have words with you afterwards you old b…" Ron stopped dead in his tracks. There was a commotion at the back of the hall. The doors had been flung open and an aggressive and openly abusive, red-faced man stood, one fist clenched, the other tightly gripping a baseball bat. Either the man was clearly drunk or had been sniffing something illegal.

"Oh my god!" Alicia grabbed Rick's hand. "I

thought he was in prison, oh Rick please don't let him spoil the day. Quickly, pass me your phone. We need to call the police now."

But there was no time to summon any police officers. The man in question was no less than a furious Jason Scott. Although it seemed in the distant past, following on from the confrontation with Alicia, Rick and Dick in the local park he had been charged and given a custodial sentence, significantly lengthened after his assaulting various police officers whilst in custody. His career and reputation in tatters, he had started his prison sentence with contempt and bitterness against those whom he felt responsible for his situation. He had escaped from prison the night before and had made it his mission to destroy those accountable for his ruined life. It had been by pure chance that he had discovered the wedding venue – Scott had been watching Alicia's house from a distance when she had been picked up by Rick and taken on to the wedding. He had made a note of the fact that Rick lived next door to his ex-girlfriend and had vowed, "You next."

There were screams from the wedding party as the baseball bat came down on the first decorated table adjacent to the doors. As the seated guests around the table fled, glassware and empty plates were strewn across the floor as the table collapsed under the force of the baseball bat. Jason looked up with a menacing smile at those seated beyond at the head table, and looking directly at Alicia shouted, "I'm gonna kill you… you bitch, and then fancy boy there, and then you, old man," looking directly at Dick, "wedding day or not." Jason advanced towards them with murderous intent, the wedding guests scattering as he advanced.

Rick wracked his brain as to how he was going to get Alicia safely out of this nutter's harm. Dick was so full of fury that the bastard was ruining Joyce's wedding day that momentarily he couldn't think straight. Then he remembered. A smile slowly spread across his face. He instructed Rick and Alicia to sit down, then took his new wife's hand and whispered into her ear, "I love you. Now please do not worry about a thing. Ron will finish his speech once Hamish has dealt with this moron. Trust me… OK?"

Although somewhat confused, at these words Joyce sat back, picked up a glass of wine and after taking a large gulp, looked at her new husband and whispered back, "I love you too."

The Reverend Hamish Dower, cool as a cucumber, arose from his seat, picked up a half-filled bottle of Rawarse Vineyards and walked slowly and defiantly towards Jason Scott as everyone else retreated from him.

"Now look here, young man, I don't know who you are or what you want, but this is hardly the way to behave at the most important day in this couple's lives. Now I don't want to hurt you, but you are starting to make me very cross!" Hamish continued to walk towards the crazed lunatic.

"Why don't you F-off you stupid old bastard!" But Jason was disturbed to see the complete lack of fear in Hamish's eyes.

"Now, stop being a naughty boy and put down the baseball bat otherwise I will be forced to crack a good bottle of Sir John's best red wine over your numbskull of a devoid brain!" Then glimpsing around momentarily at Sir John Rawarse he added, "Marvellous wine, Sir John, forgive me if I spill just this one bottle."

Sir John Rawarse raised an eyebrow and although somewhat surprised responded, "Of course, old chap. Just that one though. Be a great shame to waste any more, particularly on such a scumbag."

By now Jason was incensed with rage, but hesitated in the face of such cool and confident adversaries. The room was charged with nervous energy as all eyes followed the old padre walking confidently towards the aggressor on the far side of the hall. Then Jason snapped. Cursing obscenities, he charged, baseball bat swinging, towards the old man. Undeterred, Hamish kept calmly walking forward. It was Miss Florence Forbes's foot placed neatly in the path of the aggressor that downed the brute. Hamish was onto him like a flash. The old clergyman disarmed him of his weapon and flung it to the farthest corner of the hall. Jason regained his footing and now faced Hamish menacingly. Hamish passed the half-filled bottle of red wine to Florence. "Thank you, Florence, would you be so kind as to pour me a glass for afterwards?"

"Certainly Vicar," she responded.

"Now young man... just you and me. Are you sure you don't want to just shake hands and be done with it or must you insist on me whipping you?"

No more words from Jason Scott, just a fist that flew out with ferocity and venom towards the vicar's face. It skimmed lightly across Hamish's cheek, Jason's signet ring scratching and breaking the skin. But Hamish had ducked like a professional with the agility of a man 30 years younger, and having avoided the full force of the incoming punch, he kicked the younger man's feet from beneath him. Jason landed with a thump on the floor of the hall and then Hamish dropped like a lead weight, his knees falling onto the back of his downed opponent. The old clergyman, quick as lighting, had grabbed both his opponent's wrists and twisted them together behind the younger man's back. Jason was now completely immobile.

"Florence dear, would you be so kind as to fetch me some cord wire? It's in the kitchen, second drawer down on the right-hand side." Then, looking towards his fellow guests, "And I wonder if someone could perhaps telephone the police."

A round of applause went around the room for the Reverend Hamish Dower who had surprised, no, stunned all the guests with his combat skills and cool head. All the guests except his old comrade Dick, who knew of his skills as a black belt in karate and the fact Hamish had stood up to death many times in his military career and never been fazed. Hamish Junior had been awakened by the fracas. He tottered over to where Jason lay, tied up and no longer a threat. The puppy lifted a miniature back leg and duly pissed on the bastard, as if to say, "Serves you right for trying to ruin my new mistress's wedding day."

By the time the police had arrived, the girls of the WRVS had cleared away any debris and restored St Mary's church hall with all its wedding finery to its former glory. Hamish, Dick and Rick had helped the two responding police officers take Jason Scott to the waiting police minibus, from whence he would be escorted back to prison. Hamish had promised to visit the brute in prison, and to his friends' surprise the offer had not been rejected.

"There is always some good in everyone, and that young man just needs to find it in his heart," Hamish muttered to himself. As he returned to the church hall, a loud cheer went up and everybody broke out into spontaneous applause. Florence Forbes was the first on the scene and planted an enormous kiss on the vicar's unsuspecting lips. Hamish, in turn, thanked her for the judicious use of her outstretched foot in flooring the bastard, before giving the church organist the most amazing kiss she'd experienced since being a teenager.

Then Ron Arkwright raised a glass in honour of the brave padre to a cheering room before continuing on with his best man speech, full of amusing tales of his best friend's past antics.

It was then the bridegroom's turn to say a few words. Dick Chambers stood up and holding the hand of his new bride, started. "My dear friends… we promised you an action-packed day… but blimey, wasn't quite as I imagined it would be!"

Laughter and cheers filled the hall and Dick waited until the noise level had abated. "I… we, want to sincerely thank you all from the bottom of our hearts for your love and support, and for making this one of the happiest days of our lives. I want especially to thank the Reverend Hamish Dower, or 'Scrapper' as we used to know him!" Again there was a chorus of laughter. "I want to thank the best man, Ron, for a wonderful speech. I want to thank dearest Rick and Alicia for looking after Joyce so magnificently during her recent hospital stay. Dear friends, you know that I have had some mental health problems recently and wouldn't be here if it were not for the superb rugby tackling skills of our favourite gynaecologist, Mr Rick Donovan." The wedding guests stood in unison and applauded a rather embarrassed Rick, who modestly nodded his appreciation.

Dick continued, "In fact all the staff of our marvellous NHS should be thanked, especially the staff of Bedlam ward with us today. Needless to say Joyce and I are now most familiar with Bedlam and its fabulous staff. The ladies of the WRVS, I think you will agree have done the most amazing job today, and Sir John Rawarse… your generosity in providing wine from your own vineyards was fantastic. Thank you all." Dick then paused, composed his thoughts before finishing his brief speech of thanks. "Of course, the one person that I have not yet publicly thanked and as you know it is customary to leave the best until last, is my beloved wife, Mrs Joyce Chambers. Please raise your glasses to the woman who has made me the happiest man in the world, Joyce, darling… here's to you."

The whole room stood and toasted the new bride. As for Joyce, she couldn't remember ever feeling happier or being more content with life.

The joyous festivities in St Mary's church hall continued long into the night. Florence bashed out everyone's favourite music on the piano and a lively singsong, fuelled with goodwill and copious glasses of the finest red wine continued into the early hours.

It was just after 2am that Rick and Alicia said their 'thank-yous and goodbyes' to all concerned, with hugs and kisses, before making their excuses and leaving. As they came out of St Mary's, Rick turned to Alicia. "What an absolutely brilliant day, albeit with some interesting surprises!"

Alicia turned her head and looked at Rick. "I am

so sorry about Jason." A tear trickled down her cheek.

"My darling Alicia, don't you give it another moment's thought. In fact all this wedding business has made me think." Rick stood in front of her, then dropped to one knee. "Alicia Granger, forgive me… I don't have a ring… but this just seems right. Please would you do me the greatest honour? Would you marry me?"

"Oh Rick, I thought you'd never ask. Of course I'll marry you! Especially if you wear your hospital blues on our wedding night," she laughed.

A loud "Hurray!" was heard coming from out of the giant hydrangea shrub adjacent to the pathway leading up to St Mary's church hall. A dishevelled Reverend Hamish Dower and Florence Forbes fell out of the bush, straightened their clothing, and then proceeded to heartily congratulate the startled couple.

THE END

ABOUT THE AUTHOR

Born in South Africa, educated in England and Wales, and now living in God's own Country of Wales with his family, Sean was previously a Squadron Leader in the RAF and a GP, before retraining as a Consultant Obstetrician and Gynaecologist serving the people of the South Wales Valleys.

Sean has been a doctor for almost 30 years and his experience varies from helping out those less fortunate than us in Uganda, to facilitating IVF treatments for infertile couples.

He has previously written Medics, Minis and Mayhem (previously entitled, Diary of a Gynaecologist), which is a humorous romp about a junior doctor and the prequel to Hospital Blues. Sean has also published Infertility, IVF and Miscarriage, a self-help book for the general public, to give guidance to the 1 in 6 couples unable have their own children.

He lives in Cardiff with his wife, three children and a golden Labrador called Beano.

30656636R10153

Printed in Great
Britain
by Amazon